"Another skate," Jamie said. "And then I'm guessing it's hot chocolate?"

"That sounds utterly perfect," she said, smiling at him.

And how crazy was it that his heart suddenly felt as if it had done a backflip?

This wasn't supposed to happen. It wasn't part of their deal. They were colleagues. They weren't supposed to get close and personal.

She was the first woman since Hestia to make him feel like that. Her warmth and her huge, huge heart just drew him. Yet, at the same time, he was pretty sure that Anna was hiding some deep sadness in her own past. She deserved more than he could give her. So he forced himself to keep things light.

Until the moment when she stumbled and he caught her so she didn't fall.

She looked up at him, those beautiful sea green eyes wide and her lips very slightly parted.

And he knew then that it would be oh-so easy to dip his head slightly. Brush his mouth against hers. Wrap his arms round her, and then deepen the kiss until they were both dizzy…

Dear Reader,

Christmas can be a magical time, but for some people it's tinged with sadness. For me, Christmas was hard for a lot of years because it's very close to the anniversary of my mom's death, but having children taught me to see the joy of Christmas again.

So in Anna and Jamie's story, Anna loves Christmas but Jamie hates it. Can she teach him to see the joy again? I've used some of my favorite personal things in her campaign: seeing the Christmas lights, early school Christmas performances (which I miss terribly, now my own children are of university age—though we still have stockings and *lots* of board games and laughter), carol services and a performance of *The Nutcracker*.

I hope you enjoy their journey.

With love,

Kate Hardy

MISTLETOE PROPOSAL ON THE CHILDREN'S WARD

KATE HARDY

HARLEQUIN® MEDICAL ROMANCE™

Recycling programs
for this product may
not exist in your area.

ISBN-13: 978-1-335-64199-1

Mistletoe Proposal on the Children's Ward

First North American Publication 2019

This edition published by arrangement with Harlequin Books S.A.

For questions and comments about the quality of this book,
please contact us at CustomerService@Harlequin.com.

Printed in U.S.A.

Books by Kate Hardy

Harlequin Medical Romance

Miracles at Muswell Hill Hospital

Christmas with Her Daredevil Doc
Their Pregnancy Gift

Paddington Children's Hospital

Mommy, Nurse...Duchess?

Christmas Miracles in Maternity

The Midwife's Pregnancy Miracle

Unlocking the Italian Doc's Heart
Carrying the Single Dad's Baby
Heart Surgeon, Prince...Husband!
A Nurse and a Pup to Heal Him

Harlequin Romance

A Crown by Christmas

Soldier Prince's Secret Baby Gift

The Runaway Bride and the Billionaire
Christmas Bride for the Boss
Reunited at the Altar
A Diamond in the Snow
Finding Mr. Right in Florence

Visit the Author Profile page
at Harlequin.com for more titles.

To Gerard, Chris and Chloe, who always make
Christmas special to me

CHAPTER ONE

'HOW ARE THE ward Christmas things coming on, Anna?' Robert Jones asked.

'Brilliant, thanks.' Anna smiled at the head of the Children's Department. 'The Secret Santa is pretty much sorted, we've got Christmas dinner booked and most people have given me their deposits and menu choices, and the only thing I'm short of now is someone to be Father Christmas on Christmas Day.' Her smile broadened. 'Seeing as our usual Santa has let us down horribly.'

Robert held up both hands in a 'stop' gesture and laughed. 'Anna, you know why I can't do it this year. I'd have to fly back from New York. And that's more than my life is worth, on my silver wedding anniversary.'

'Even for the ward? Even for me?' she teased.

'Even for the ward and even for you,' Robert said. 'Actually, Anna, I did want to ask you a bit of a favour. Jamie Thurston—the new paediatric orthopod who's covering Nalini's maternity leave for the first three months—is joining us today.'

'And you want me to show him around and help him settle in?' Anna guessed.

'Would you?' Robert asked.

'Of course.' She smiled at him again. 'I'm in the PAU this morning. I'll leave a message with whoever is on the desk to ask him to meet me at one and I'll take him to lunch.'

'Great.' Robert patted her shoulder. 'Thank you.'

'Pleasure,' Anna said, and had a quick word with Lacey on the reception desk before she headed for the Paediatric Assessment Unit.

Her third patient of the day was a four-month-old baby who had been referred to her clinic by the health visitor, on the grounds of possible DDH—developmental dysplasia of the hip. A quick read through the notes ticked all the boxes of a higher risk: Poppy Byford was a first baby, a girl, born at thirty-six weeks and had been in the breech position. So Anna was pretty sure that the health visitor had picked up the problem.

'Good morning, Ms Byford. Do come in and let's have a look at Poppy,' Anna said. 'Hello, you gorgeous girl.' She cooed at the baby, who giggled and waved her hands. 'She's beautiful,' Anna said, and stuffed the little twinge of longing right back down out of the way. She could enjoy being an aunt and enjoy working with her young patients, and that was enough. Wanting more was greedy and pointless—and the quickest way to get her heart broken.

'Thank you.' Poppy's mum looked nervous.

'Your health visitor asked you to bring Poppy to see me because she thinks Poppy might have something called developmental dysplasia of the hip—you might hear it called DDH for short, or "clicky hip",' Anna explained. 'Usually it shows up in a newborn examination, and I can see in Poppy's notes that the doctor did a hip test at her six-week check and it seemed normal. But the health visitor's concerned and wants me to do another check.'

'Is Poppy going to be all right?' Ms Byford asked. 'I did start looking it up on the Internet, but…' She grimaced.

'The Internet is a very scary place where

medical problems conditions are concerned,' Anna said. 'It's like when you're pregnant with your first child, and you always hear the horror stories about difficult labours rather than the smooth ones, even though the difficult ones are much rarer. There is a possibility that Poppy might grow out of the condition, but I'd like to examine her properly and then do an ultrasound scan to check how her hip is developing.' She smiled. 'I promise what I do isn't going to hurt her, but she might not appreciate being manipulated and might grumble a bit.'

'All right,' Ms Byford said.

'Have you noticed when you change her nappy that one hip doesn't open out quite as much as the other?' Anna asked.

Ms Byford wrinkled her nose. 'Not really. I thought everything was normal. I mean— she's my only one.'

'So you don't have anything to compare her with. That's fine.' Anna gave her a reassuring smile. 'Could you take her tights off for me, please?'

Once Ms Byford had taken the tights off the baby, Anna examined Poppy and cooed at her while she manipulated the baby's joints, blowing raspberries to make her laugh.

'So do you think she has this clicky hip thing?' Ms Byford asked.

'I felt a bit of a clunk when I moved her legs just now, so yes,' Anna said. 'I can see that her right leg is slightly shorter than the left, and basically I think her thigh bone isn't moving properly in the socket of her pelvis. We'll do the scan, and then we can think about treatment. It might be that we do a watch-and-wait thing, or we might put her in a special harness to treat the hip dysplasia, but I'll be in a better position to know what'll work best once I've seen the scan results. And the scan's like the one you had when you were pregnant with her, so it won't hurt,' she added reassuringly.

While Poppy was having her scan, Anna saw her next patient. The scan results definitely showed a problem with Poppy's hip, but whether the harness would be enough or the baby would need treatment with traction, she wasn't sure.

'I'm going to have a word with one of my colleagues,' she said to Ms Byford. 'He's a specialist in children's bones, and I'd like to check a couple of things with him. I'm sorry,

I'm afraid it means a bit more waiting about for you, but please try not to worry because this really is something we can sort out for Poppy.'

To her relief, the new paediatric orthopod was in one of the offices, reviewing notes for his operating list the next day. She rapped on the open door. 'Mr Thurston?' she asked. 'I'm Anna Maskell, one of the special regs on the ward, and I've got a baby with clicky hip. She's a borderline case and I'm not sure if she needs an op, so would you mind reviewing her scan and treatment plan with me, please?'

'Sure,' he said, looking up from his notes.

His eyes were the most piercing cornflower blue, and Anna felt her pulse leap.

How completely inappropriate.

For a start, they were at work, and her patients always came first. Secondly, given that Jamie Thurston looked to be in his mid-thirties, he was probably already involved with someone; but, even if he wasn't, Anna wasn't looking for a relationship. Love wasn't on her list of things to do, not any more. It had taken her two years to put her heart back together since Johnny's affair and the disintegration of her marriage, and she wasn't planning to risk her heart breaking ever again.

'Thank you. Robert asked me earlier if I would show you around,' she added. 'I was due in the Paediatric Assessment Unit before you arrived, so I asked Lacey to pass on a message inviting you to lunch, as it's your first day and you probably haven't had a chance to find your way around yet.'

So this was Anna Maskell, the woman who'd left him that kind message, Jamie thought.

She was taller than average with broad shoulders, a shock of dark curly hair she'd tied back at the nape of her neck, and eyes the same green as the sea on a summer day; she was more like an Artemis than a delicate nymph, though it shocked him he was even thinking that way. For a moment, his tongue felt as if it had stuck to the roof of his mouth. Then he pulled himself together. 'Yes, she did tell me. Thank you. That was kind.'

'Pleasure. My patient?' She sounded businesslike, but kind rather than snippy.

'Of course.' He logged out of his screen and shifted his chair so she could draw up the scan for her patient.

'Poppy Byford is four months old,' Anna said. 'She has all the risk factors for DDH, but her newborn and six-week checks were completely normal. The health visitor was concerned that one hip wasn't opening out properly and referred her. I definitely felt a clunk when I manipulated her legs, and I don't think watch-and-wait is the right way forward for her, but I'm not sure whether to try a Pavlik harness for a couple of months or whether traction would be a better option—I'm hoping we might be able to get away without an operation, but I could really do with an orthopod's view. As I said, she's borderline.'

Jamie liked the way she was so clear in giving him the information he needed to help him make the clinical decision—and that she'd clearly thought the treatment options through before coming to see him.

'I agree, it looks borderline,' he said. 'As she's younger than six months, I agree that it would be better to start with something less invasive than an operation. Let's try a harness for three months,' he suggested, 'and we can give an ultrasound review of how her hips are developing every month.'

'Great. Thank you.' She smiled at him.

How strange that a smile could almost make him feel warm inside.

He hadn't felt warm since Hestia had died, three years ago.

Before he realised what he was doing, Jamie found himself looking at Anna's left hand. Ridiculous. Apart from the fact that not wearing a ring didn't mean she wasn't already committed elsewhere, he wasn't looking to get involved with anyone. No way could he face the emptiness of losing someone again and having to try to put his life back together again afterwards.

Work.

This was strictly work. End of.

'Would you like me to come and talk to Poppy's mum and fit the harness?' he asked.

'Would you mind?'

'Sure. I was only reviewing tomorrow's list, and that can wait. I'll come now.'

In the assessment unit, Anna introduced him swiftly to Poppy and her mum.

'The good news is,' Jamie said, 'we're not necessarily looking at an operation to help Poppy's hips. We can fit something called a Pavlik harness; it will keep her hips in the right position so they can develop properly.'

'Will it hurt?' Ms Byford asked.

'No. It's lightweight and made of fabric,' Anna said. 'You might find it a bit upsetting to see it, and Poppy might be a bit grizzly for the first few days, but it won't hurt her and she'll soon get used to it.'

'She'll need to wear it all the time,' Jamie added. 'It will be easier for you to put her in loose clothes while she's got the harness fitted.'

'Do I take it off when she has a bath?' Ms Byford asked.

'No. Just top and tail her rather than giving her a full bath,' Jamie said. 'We'll see you every week to adjust the harness as she grows, and she can have a proper bath here when we take the harness off, before we do the adjustment.'

'So how long will she have to wear this harness?' Ms Byford asked.

'Maybe for two or three months,' Jamie said. 'We'll give Poppy an ultrasound scan every month to see how her hips are developing, and you'll see a physiotherapist with her here every week.'

Ms Byford frowned. 'What if the harness gets dirty?'

'The harness can be sponge cleaned,' Anna said. 'And some of my parents have put long socks over the baby's legs to protect the harness during nappy changes.' She smiled. 'One of my mums calls them the "poo socks".'

Ms Byford looked close to tears. 'Only a few days ago, everything was fine. And now...'

'The good news is that Poppy might not need an operation,' Jamie said gently. 'And a harness is a lot easier to manage than a plaster cast. Hopefully, wearing the harness will encourage her joints to develop as they should. I know this has been a shock to you, but she's going to be fine. The earlier we pick up something like this, the quicker it is to treat.'

'And she'll be all right?' Ms Byford asked.

'She'll be absolutely fine,' Anna reassured her. 'I know right now it feels as if you don't know anyone else going through this and it's a bit daunting, but Poppy's not the only baby I've seen with clicky hip, and all my former patients with it have gone through treatment and are just the same as their peers now. The next thing you know, Poppy will be crawling and you'll be shocked at just how fast a determined baby can move.'

Between them, Jamie and Anna fitted the harness. Poppy protested, and her mum watched them with silent tears rolling down her cheeks, looking anxious.

Anna gave her a reassuring hug. 'I know right now it feels a bit scary and overwhelming, but you'll both get used to it and she'll be back to her usual smiley self before you know it. I'll book you in with the physiotherapist and my clinic for a week's time, and in the meantime if you've got any questions just ring in.' She took a leaflet from a drawer. 'This will tell you all about the harness and what it does, if anyone asks you and it's gone all fuzzy because right now you're worrying too much about Poppy to take everything in.'

Jamie glanced at her. Anna Maskell was kind as well as professional. And he could already see the difference that kindness had made to the patient's mother; Ms Byford had stopped crying and was asking questions.

Anna, he thought, was going to be good to work with.

Not that he intended getting close to her or to any of his other colleagues in the Muswell Hill Memorial Hospital. He'd agreed to cover maternity leave here for three months, and that was all. He didn't need to make new friends. He was absolutely fine on his own.

'All the best, Ms Byford. I'll see you later, Dr Maskell,' he said. And he left the room before he was tempted to blow a raspberry at Poppy and make the baby laugh.

Babies.

How ironic that this was his vocation, the job he loved so much.

After losing Hestia and the baby, Jamie hadn't wanted to see another baby or child ever again. But he wasn't going to throw all those years of hard work and studying away and change his career. Hestia would never have forgiven him for that. But, unable to face the pity of his team at the hospital where he'd worked in south London, he'd switched to working as a locum. No involvement, no closeness, no risk of heartache. He stayed for no longer than three months in one place; as soon as his locum cover was finished, he moved on to the next job. That was how his life had been for the last two and a half years, and that was how he intended it to stay. Utterly within his comfort zone.

Anna finished writing up her notes for the last patient of her morning's clinic, then headed to the office where she'd met Jamie Thurston earlier. 'Ready?' she asked from the doorway.

'Yes.' He logged out of the files he'd been reviewing, then came to join her.

'Did Robert introduce you to everyone when you started this morning, or would you like to meet everyone now?'

'Robert introduced me,' Jamie said.

'That's great. OK. I'm assuming he also showed you the staff kitchen?'

'Yes.'

'Just the canteen, then,' she said, 'and filling you in on the social side of the ward.'

'Social side?'

Was it her imagination, or did Jamie look a bit antsy? 'We're a close team. We do a lot of things together outside work,' she said. 'And we try to do stuff that includes partners and children.'

He said nothing, simply nodded.

'Locums count as part of the team,' she said softly. But she shut up when she noticed his slight frown. Maybe he was shy. And it was his first day on the team, so she should cut him some slack.

She left it until they'd bought lunch and found a quiet table in the canteen. 'I guess it's because I have bossy tendencies,' she said, smiling to take the sting from her words, 'but I organise most of the ward's social stuff. I've had the venue for the team Christmas dinner booked since July, but I don't have to give the absolute final numbers or confirm everyone's menu choices to the pub for another week or so.'

Jamie's wrap stopped tasting like sweet chilli chicken and turned to ashes in his mouth.

Christmas.

No.

Since Hestia's death, he didn't do Christmas. There weren't tidings of comfort and joy, as far as he was concerned. Just the bleak midwinter, and the radio playing songs saying how it would be lonely at Christmas, or begging the singer's loved one to come home for Christmas, or, worse still, the song Hestia had loved and danced around the house to with him, making him sing along with her. The most popular modern song, the one that seemed to be playing all the time in December, no matter which radio station he chose.

All Hestia had wanted for Christmas was him. And their baby.

That was what he'd wanted, too.

What he'd actually got was a double funeral. All those plans, all the happiness and excitement, had sunk into a black hole. It was just over three years ago now, and everyone had expected him to move on. But he couldn't. It was too, too hard.

Which was why he worked as a locum.

And why he flatly refused social invitations from family and friends alike, since the time they'd all clearly talked about him and decided he needed help to move on, and had set him up at a dinner party with a suitably single woman. A nice, sweet woman who deserved so much more than the wreckage that had once been Jamie Thurston. He'd been polite, the first couple of times it had happened, but then he'd refused invitations so he wouldn't be put in an awkward position again. He didn't need to be fixed up with anyone. He didn't want anyone else in his life.

'Sorry. I don't think—' he began, but Anna had already fished her phone out of her pocket.

'It's very much a foodie pub, so the food's utterly amazing,' she said. 'The smoked salmon pâté is to die for.'

Die. Yeah. Jamie knew all about dying and

death. Though this wasn't Anna's fault. She didn't know him, so she'd have no idea how inappropriate that phrase was.

'If you're veggie or vegan, the avocado on toast with chilli jam is fantastic. Or the spiced pumpkin soup,' she continued.

He didn't want to even think about a ward Christmas dinner, let alone go to one.

'They do the best roast potatoes in the world—better even than my mum's, which is saying a lot,' she said. 'Crispy on the outside and fluffy in the middle. And they stir-fry the Brussels sprouts with lemon and chilli. There's traditional turkey, sea bass if you pre-fer fish, or parsnip and chestnut Wellington for the veggie/vegan option.' She passed her phone to him so he could see the menu for himself. 'Obviously there's traditional Christ-mas pudding or cheese, but I guarantee the chocolate Venetian cake will ruin you for any other pudding.'

He blinked at her.

'Or I can email everything over to you, if you want to take a bit of time choosing. It's the first Friday evening in December, at half-past seven,' she said. 'And we do a Secret Santa on the ward, too—you pick a name out of the hat, leave your labelled parcel with the secretaries, and Robert puts the ward's Father Christmas outfit on and dishes them out on the night. Anyone who can't make it to the dinner gets their parcel at the start of their next shift.'

This was going way, way too fast for him.

She gave him a speculative look. 'Actually… Robert usually dresses up as Father Christmas for us on the ward on Christmas Day, but this year he's disappearing off to New York.' She smiled. 'I guess his silver wedding anniversary's a good enough excuse for him not to do it this year. But it means I need a replacement Father Christmas. You're about the same height as Robert, so the costume would fit you perfectly.'

What? Jamie could barely process this. She wanted him to dress up as Father Christmas?

He couldn't.

He just *couldn't*.

Finally, he found his voice. 'Sorry. I can't.'

Something must've shown in his eyes, because she winced. 'I'm so sorry. This is only your first day, and I'm overwhelming you. Let me backtrack a bit. I'll send you all the stuff about the ward Christmas events, but maybe you'd like to come ten-pin bowling with the team on Friday night as a starter? It'll give you a chance to meet people you might not have met on the ward yet, and we're a nice lot. Not everyone's as…um…steamrollery as me.'

Steamrollery? Yes, she was. But the woman he'd seen on the ward was also kind. She gave patients and their parents time to think about things, and made sure they had all the information they needed so they knew all the facts and could make a good decision about their healthcare plan. She tried to understand their feelings. Yes, she'd overwhelmed him a bit just now, but that was probably just because he hated Christmas.

'I haven't been ten-pin bowling in years,' he said.

'It doesn't matter if you're a bit rusty. I cheat hideously and keep the bumper bars up in my lane,' she confided, 'because I can't bowl in a straight line. Straight to the gutter every time, that's me.' She rolled her eyes. 'Sadly, being tall and built like an Amazon doesn't mean that I'm any good at sport.'

He wanted to refuse the invitation and tell her he didn't do social stuff.

But her smile disarmed him. It was warm and friendly and ever so slightly goofy, and it shocked him that she could affect him this way. He'd kept his distance from everyone for nearly three years. How could a near-stranger make him feel…?

'It's all just a bit of fun, and nobody takes things seriously,' she said. 'It's a chance for everyone to let off a bit of steam and enjoy each other's company. Thankfully nobody on the ward is one of those competitive idiots who just *have* to win all the time; everyone's really nice.'

Nice. That usually went with kindness. And if his new colleagues found out about his past they'd swamp him in pity. Jamie really, really couldn't handle that. He'd had more than enough pity to last him a lifetime. He just wanted to be left alone.

'Thanks for inviting me,' he said, fully intending to make an excuse and say that he couldn't make it.

But then the wrong words came out of his mouth, shocking him. 'I'll be there.'

What? He didn't do social stuff.

But it was too late, because she was already looking thrilled that he'd agreed to join them. 'Fantastic. We normally grab something to eat at the bowling alley, too—I'm afraid it's not the greatest nutrition because it's pretty much a choice of pizza, nachos or burger and fries, but it's edible. Our lanes are booked at seven,' she said. 'I'm assuming that you're new to the area, so I'll send you directions.'

It was definitely too late to back out now. Or maybe he could invent a last-minute emergency on Friday night and just not go.

'Let me have your number and your email,' she said, 'and I'll send you everything.'

That smile again. Its warmth melted Jamie's reluctance, and he found himself giving Anna his number and his email address. A moment or so later, his phone pinged to signify an incoming message.

'So now you have my number, and I'll send you all the rest of the stuff after work,' she said. 'Welcome to Muswell Hill Memorial Hospital, Jamie.'

CHAPTER TWO

HEADACHE? JAMIE THOUGHT on Friday night. No, because that could be easily fixed with a couple of paracetamol. Bubonic plague? Strictly speaking, that did still exist, but the last case he'd heard of had been in Colorado and that wasn't quite near enough to London to be plausible; plus if the condition was diagnosed properly it could be cured by the right antibiotic. Held up in traffic? No, because the bowling alley was within walking distance of his flat.

He didn't have a single believable excuse not to turn up to the team night out.

He did have Anna's number, so he could just call her and admit that he didn't want to go. But it felt too mean-spirited and he couldn't quite bring himself to do it.

And so he found himself outside the bowling alley at five minutes to seven. There was

a group of people he recognised in the foyer;
Anna detached herself from them and came
over to greet him. 'Hey, Jamie! Glad you could
make it.'

He'd seen her several times at work during the week, wearing a smart shirt and skirt
beneath her white coat. In jeans and a long-
sleeved T-shirt, and with her dark wavy hair
loose, she looked very different: younger and
very, very approachable. He was suddenly
aware of her curves and how the faded denim
clung to her.

Oh, for pity's sake. He wasn't a hormone-
laden teenager. He'd seen plenty of women
dressed casually.

But they didn't make him feel suddenly hot
all over, the way Anna Maskell did.

Tonight was *definitely* a mistake. Even if
she wasn't involved with someone, he was
only here in Muswell Hill for three months,
and then he'd move on. He wasn't in the market for a relationship, even a temporary one.
He could never give his heart again. He'd buried his capacity to love right there in the grave
with his wife and his daughter.

But he forced himself to smile back. To fake
a semblance of being a normal member of the

team. He let her introduce him to the people he hadn't yet met from their ward, swapped his shoes for bowling shoes, paid for his games, and chipped in his share of the food and drink order. He played the frames along with the rest of the team, sitting squarely in the middle of the scoring and being neither spectacularly good nor spectacularly bad.

Though Anna was playing on his lane, and she'd been right on the money when she'd told him that she was terrible at bowling. Without the bumper bars being put up, her ball would've gone straight into the gutter every single time; as it was, she seemed to have a strategy of zig-zagging the ball between the sides of the lane in the hope of hitting the pins in the middle, more by luck than by judgement.

'Yes! Six pins! Best roll of the night for me so far,' she whooped as the pins went down.

'Best roll of the last four years, by my count,' one of the others teased.

'I know! How cool is that?' She punched the air and then grinned. 'Go, me.'

Everyone else on the team high-fived her, so Jamie felt he had to follow suit.

But when the palm of his hand grazed

briefly against hers, it felt like an electric shock.

He was pretty sure she felt it, too, because those beautiful sea-green eyes widened briefly. And for a second it felt as if it was just the two of them in a bubble: the sound of bowling balls thudding against pins on the other lanes, of the electronic scoreboard, of music playing and people laughing and talking, simply melted away.

Then he shook himself. This wasn't happening. Anna was his colleague for the next few weeks, and then he'd be moving on.

But he couldn't shift his awareness of her. The tall, energetic, human dynamo of their department. The woman who was definitely attracting him, despite his common sense.

When their food order arrived, they took a break, and Jamie found himself sitting next to Anna. His fingers accidentally brushed against hers as they reached for a piece of pizza at the same time, and again it felt like an electric shock. He was going to have to be really careful.

'So have you had a chance to look at the Christmas menu yet?' she asked.

The Christmas meal he really didn't want to go to. 'Sorry, no.'

She looked disappointed. 'Well, we've still got a bit of time,' she said. 'And maybe I can talk you into being Father Christmas for me.'

He shook his head. 'Sorry. Absolutely not.'

'Don't tell me—you're allergic to red suits and big white beards?'

If she'd been pushy or snippy or sarcastic, it would've been easy to resist. To push back. But this, the jokiness underlain by a sweetness—this was much harder to resist.

He was going to have to tell her the truth.

'I really don't like Christmas,' he said, and waited for her to start probing.

To his surprise, she didn't.

'A lot of people find Christmas hard,' she said. 'And it's really rough on our patients and their parents. The patients who are old enough to want to be home with their families and are still young enough to believe in Father Christmas all want to know if that's what he'll give them: the chance to go home for Christmas. I hate telling them he can't do that. The ones who are too old to believe in Father Christmas—for them it's seeing their families and knowing how much it hurts them to be apart at Christmas, especially when they're trying to juggle family celebrations with hospital visits and kind of splitting themselves in two. Christmas can be horrible.'

The way she said it made him realise how she felt. 'But you don't think it is?'

'No. I love Christmas,' she said. 'I love the way it breaks down barriers and makes people kinder to each other, if only for a few hours. And I love the look of wonder in our younger patients' faces when Father Christmas strides onto the ward, saying, "Ho-ho-ho," and hands them a special gift from the Friends of the Hospital. It's nothing hugely expensive, usually a book or some art stuff or a teddy bear, but enough to show them that Christmas in hospital isn't completely bad. I bring my guitar in and we sing a few Christmassy songs; being part of that is just amazing. Despite all the worry and the fear, there's still hope and love.'

Hope and love. Things he'd lost a long time ago.

'I'm sorry for being pushy. I completely understand that you'd rather not be Father Christmas.' She gave him a wry smile. 'It's really starting to look as if it's going to be Mother Christmas this year.'

He suddenly realised what she was getting at. '*You're* going to dress up in the Santa suit?'

'I haven't been able to talk anyone else into it,' she said, 'so it's either no Father Christmas at all, or me. I guess at least I'm tall enough to get away with it.' She spread her hands and grinned. 'I might be able to borrow a voice-changer from my nephew or someone and hide it behind the beard. That, or I'm going to be channelling a Shakespearean actor and learning how to do a deep, booming voice.'

Anna Maskell was tall, yes, but there was nothing remotely masculine about her. She wouldn't convince anyone that she was Father Christmas.

Jamie knew he should be nice and offer to help. But he just couldn't get the words out.

Why did Jamie Thurston dislike Christmas so much? Anna wondered.

Maybe he'd had a difficult childhood, one where his family had rowed all the time and Christmas just made things worse—people being forced together for longer periods of time than they could stand each other. The

Emergency Department was testament to how bad Christmas tensions could get. Add alcohol to the mix, and it was often explosive and painful.

But it would be rude and intrusive to ask.

She switched the conversation to something lighter. 'There's a team football thing in the park next weekend. Partners and children included, if you'd all like to come along.'

'No children and no partner,' he said, and the bleakness in his eyes shocked her.

Maybe he was divorced, and his former partner had moved away so he never got to see the children. In which case it was no wonder that he didn't like Christmas. The festive season was a time for children, and not being able to see your kids at Christmas must be like rubbing salt into a very raw wound.

'Sorry. I wasn't trying to pry. Or to come on to you,' she added, realising that he might have taken her words the wrong way.

And she really wasn't trying to come on to him. Yes, Jamie Thurston was gorgeous; he reminded her of the actor in one of her favourite historical dramas, all dark and brooding and with those amazing cornflower-blue eyes. But she wasn't risking her heart again. Johnny had made it very clear that nobody would want to tie themselves down to her, not once they knew the truth about her. She was pretty sure he'd said it to make himself feel better; the man she'd fallen in love with had been one of the good guys, but the shock of learning that they couldn't have a family without a lot of medical intervention had changed him. It had made him look elsewhere; and then the guilt of knowing how badly he'd treated Anna had pushed him into saying unforgivable things that had hurt her even more than his betrayal.

'I'm just not very good at social things,' Jamie said.

'Though the football isn't a Christmassy thing.' She winced even as the words spilled out of her mouth. Oh, for pity's sake. The poor man had made it quite clear that he didn't want to do the team thing next week. Why didn't she take the hint and just get off his case?

Thankfully then their session on the bowling lanes started again, and she had to concentrate on trying to make the ball go straight. Not that she managed it. And this time she only knocked down one pin from each end. How pathetic was that?

Jamie said to her, 'It's your follow-through.'

'Follow-through?' she asked, mystified.

'Where your hand points, that's where the ball ends up.'

She laughed wryly. 'Straight in the gutter, if I didn't have the bumper bars up. But I guess my zig-zag approach is a bit too haphazard.'

'Keep your arm straight and let the ball go when your hand's pointing to the middle of the pins,' he said. 'Watch me.'

She did. 'Wow. You got a strike.'

'Because I aimed for the middle.'

'*I* aim for the middle,' she protested.

'But you let the ball go too late,' he said. 'I take it you don't go ten-pin bowling with your partner?'

Johnny hadn't really been into ten-pin bowling. 'No partner,' she said.

He winced. 'That wasn't a come-on.'

'I know.' She smiled at him. 'You sounded like someone who wants to help. A friend. And I appreciate that.'

He stilled, and she wondered if she'd gone too far.

But then he smiled. The kind of smile that lit up the whole room, and it transformed him utterly. It was as if he'd stepped out of the shadows he seemed to keep round him. When he smiled, Jamie Maskell was breathtakingly handsome.

'I'll help you with the next frame,' he said.

'Whatever you do, I'm still going to come last on our lane,' she warned. 'But it would be nice to actually do this right, for once.'

'I can help you do that.'

She looked at him. 'You're like me, aren't you? A fixer at heart.'

'It's kind of the definition of a surgeon, fixing things,' he said dryly.

It was more than that, she thought. He was a fixer who wasn't going to admit it.

Whatever had made Jamie Thurston put distance between himself and the world—and between himself and Christmas—maybe she could help him with that, the way he was helping her with the bowling.

She thought about it while they chatted with the others in their lane.

She stopped thinking for a little while when Jamie helped her with the bowling, standing close to her but not close enough to be sleazy or awkward. Because then he slid his arm along hers, showing her how to angle the ball correctly. The touch of his skin against his flustered her so much that she nearly forgot to let the ball go.

'You went slightly to the left,' he said when she'd knocked six pins down. 'So this time you need to go slightly to the right.'

Again, he guided her through the procedure. And this time her ball hit the four pins in the middle, and they all went down.

'There you go. You got a half-strike.'

'That's *amazing*.' She flung her arms round him and hugged him.

When was the last time anyone had hugged him? When he'd actually *let* a woman hug him, because he'd pushed his mum and his sisters away, not to mention Hestia's family and her best friend?

Probably at the funeral.

And now Anna Maskell had ignored all his usual barriers and hugged him. Briefly, because she stepped back almost immediately and said, 'Sorry. That was a bit over the top. But I don't think I've ever managed to get all the pins down like that before and I got a bit overexcited.' She took a deep breath. 'Let me be more appropriate. Thank you for your help, Mr Thurston,' she said more formally.

'You're most welcome, Dr Maskell,' he replied, equally formally. Though he could feel himself withdrawing again. Going back into the dark little hole where he'd lived for the last three years. But that hug had made him feel odd. As if there was a little flare of light, far in the distance. A light that drew him and beckoned him—if he had the courage to go and find it.

It took enough courage for him simply to exist from day to day. Going in search of a new life still felt too hard. But now he knew it was out there, and the little light wasn't going to let itself hide again. It stayed put, telling him it would still be there when he was ready to look for it properly.

He managed to focus on the bowling for the rest of the evening. But then it was over, everyone was spilling outside, and his new colleagues all seemed to be heading off in different directions.

He'd walked a few steps when he realised that Anna was beside him. 'It looks as if we're going the same way,' she said. 'Do you mind if I walk with you?'

'That's fine.'

'Thank you for the bowling lesson,' she said.

'Pleasure.' The word was polite and automatic, but Jamie was shocked to realise that he actually meant it. He'd enjoyed helping Anna, seeing her confidence grow along with her ability.

She'd said that she thought he was a fixer at heart.

He had been, once. Before the thing had happened that he hadn't been able to fix. And he had to admit that it had been good to feel that way again, however briefly.

'I was thinking,' she said. 'Maybe I can help you.'

He frowned. 'How?'

'Christmas,' she said.

The time of year he really disliked.

'This isn't a come-on,' she added. 'Just to be clear, I'm not looking to date anyone.'

She'd said earlier that she didn't have a partner; though Jamie could imagine Anna Maskell right at the heart of a family. A large one. Why didn't she have a partner, and why didn't she want to date anyone?

Though it was none of his business and he wasn't going to ask; if he started asking personal questions, then it was tantamount to an invitation for other people to ask him the same sort of things. Things he didn't want to discuss.

'I'm not going to pry,' she said, echoing his own thoughts. 'But Christmas is a fairly big thing at Muswell Hill Memorial Hospital, so it's going to be in your face all the time. Maybe I can help show you that Christmas has its good side, so you don't feel you have to try to avoid it all the time and it makes life feel a bit less pants at work.'

Maybe he should tell her why he disliked Christmas, so she'd back off.

Then again, he didn't want to see the pity in her face once he told her what had happened.

'Show me that Christmas has its good side,' he echoed.

'Yes. And, just in case you think I'm pitying you, I will admit that I have an ulterior motive.'

He frowned. 'Doesn't that kind of ruin any scheming, if you warn me that you have an ulterior motive?'

'No,' she said, 'because I believe in what you see is what you get.'

He was going to have to ask now. 'What's your ulterior motive?'

'I help you, and you help me.'

Oh, no. He knew exactly where this was going. 'You mean, if you show me that Christmas isn't the worst time of the year, then I'll play Father Christmas for the ward?'

She grinned. 'Thank you, Jamie. That's an offer I'm very happy to accept.'

Hang on. He hadn't offered. He'd just said out loud what he was pretty sure she was thinking. 'But I—' He couldn't finish the sentence. She'd shocked him into silence.

'Sometimes,' she said gently, 'when you avoid something, you give it more power than it deserves. Facing it head-on can cut it back down to its proper size and make it manageable again.'

He didn't have an answer to that.

'I've had days when I've had to fake it to make it,' she said. 'Days when I haven't wanted to get out of bed and face the world—days when all I've wanted to do is curl into a little ball and let it all wash over me.'

He knew exactly how that felt, and it made him look at her. *Really* look at her. And there wasn't any pity in her expression. Just empathy. Understanding. Clearly someone or something had hurt her enough that she'd been through an emotional nightmare, too.

'I'm not going to pry,' she said, 'but I think Christmas is like that for you. I'm a fixer, just like I think you are. I can't fix everything, and neither can you. But I reckon we might be able to fix a problem for each other, because we're on the same team.'

Of course she couldn't fix his problem. Nobody could bring anyone back from the dead.

He was about to say no. But then he remembered this evening. How she'd steamrollered him into joining in with the ten-pin bowling, and he'd actually ended up enjoying the evening. He'd felt part of a group of people—something he'd told himself he never wanted to do again. But that momentary closeness had managed to do what he'd thought was impossible; it had temporarily lifted the cloak of misery from round him.

If she could take the bits he hated about Christmas away, too, then maybe this was worth a shot. And if she could do that, he'd very happily wear that Father Christmas outfit to help her in return. 'So what exactly are you suggesting?' he asked.

'Doing Christmassy things together,' she said. 'It's the middle of November now. Give me a month. If I can convince you that Christmas has its good side, then you agree to be Father Christmas for the ward.'

'And if you can't convince me?'

'Then there's a bit of padding and a voice-changer in my very near future,' she said. 'And I'll also apologise for not being able to make this time of year more bearable for you.'

He could walk away now. Stay wrapped in his shroud of misery.

Or he could say yes.

Anna had made it clear that she wasn't asking him because she fancied him. The pull of attraction he felt towards her was clearly one-sided, and he had no intention of acting upon it anyway. She was merely suggesting that they could help each other.

He could almost hear Hestia's voice in his ear. *Say yes.* The petite ballet teacher he'd fallen in love with had adored Christmas. She'd loved all the snowflakes and the fairy lights and the joy that her favourite ballet brought to her students and their parents alike. He'd loved it as much as she had, because her joy had been infectious.

Without her, it had been unbearable and he'd avoided it.

He had to admit it would be good to be able to cope with Christmas again. To remember the joy Hestia had found in the festive season, instead of seeing it as a harsh reminder of everything he'd lost. And for him to stop putting a dampener on Christmas for his family, choosing to work and stay out of the way instead of spending any time with them or inflicting his misery on them during the festive season. He knew they all worried about him.

'All right,' he said. 'You're on.'

'Thank you. And you can start by texting me your menu choices for the ward's Christmas meal over the weekend,' she said. Though her smile wasn't full of triumph; instead it was a mixture of relief and gratitude. 'Maybe we can begin with something light and easy. There's a Winter Festival in the park for the next three weeks—basically it's a big Christmas market. Are you working on Sunday?'

'No.'

'Good. I'm on an early shift, so I'll meet you at four o'clock by the park gates.' She stopped outside a gate. 'This is me. I'll see you on Sunday. And thank you.'

'See you on Sunday,' he echoed.

CHAPTER THREE

FOUR NEW BRONCHIOLITIS CASES, Anna thought with a sigh on Sunday afternoon. This was peak season for the respiratory syncytial virus. In adults, it produced a spectacularly nasty cold, but in children it could be much more serious, gumming up the tiny tubes inside their lungs and making it hard for them to breathe.

Small babies often went on to develop pneumonia as a result, and Anna really felt for both her tiny patients and their parents, who were often exhausted with worry and shocked by the sight of their little ones on oxygen and being fed by a tube down their nose because the babies were too tired to suck milk from a breast or a bottle.

She finished writing up her notes, did a last check on the ward in case anyone needed emergency help before she left, then texted

Jamie to let him know that she was leaving the hospital on time and would meet him at four.

Hopefully she could change his views on Christmas and take away its power to hurt him. She wasn't going to pry and ask exactly why he hated Christmas so much, but it would be good to think that she could make life a bit better for him.

Anna the Fixer. Her whole family teased her about it, but she knew they appreciated what she did. Her own problem wasn't fixable, but you couldn't have everything. She was blessed with a wonderful family and good friends, and she'd just about forgiven Johnny for the way he'd thrown their marriage away, even though part of her still thought that there were ways round her infertility; they could've given IVF a try, or fostering or adoption. But Johnny had found the pressure and the worry too much to cope with, and he'd chosen someone who could give him what he wanted without the complications.

It was just a pity that he hadn't ended their marriage before he'd found that someone else.

His betrayal had made everything feel so much worse; and for months after that Anna had felt herself not good enough for anyone. Especially when Johnny had sneered at her that nobody would want her because she wasn't a real woman and couldn't give a man the family he wanted. She knew it had probably been guilt talking, trying to justify the way he'd treated her; before she'd married him, if anyone had told her he'd ever be so cruel to her in the future she would have laughed, not believing it. She and Johnny had loved each other, and they'd been happy.

But her infertility had shattered his dreams as well as her own; the months and months of disappointment when they'd tried and failed to make a baby had made him bitter, and he just hadn't been able to cope. In turn, that had made him feel less of a man, and the anger and guilt had spilled over into spite towards the person who was causing the problem in the first place.

It had taken a long time for Anna to get her bounce back after the split. As she'd said to Jamie earlier, she'd really had to fake it until she'd managed to make it. But she *had* made it, and she wasn't going to let herself slip back into misery.

'Don't start whining and wanting things you can't have, Anna Maskell,' she told herself firmly. 'You're really lucky and your life is as perfect as it gets. You have a family you love and who loves you all the way back, you're working in your dream job, and you have wonderful colleagues you get on really well with. You can afford to pay your rent and put food on the table. You're healthy.' Well, apart from one thing, but she wasn't actually sick with it. Infertility had just changed her options, that was all. 'You're so much more fortunate than a lot of people. And with your working hours it wouldn't be fair to have a dog, so George the Gorgeous Goldfish is enough for you.'

The line from the old song about the doggie in the window slid into her head. But it was pointless regretting that she couldn't take George for a walk in the park. There were plenty of dogs in her family that she could go and cuddle, and children she could play with. She needed to count her blessings, not dwell on the things she couldn't have.

As for dating again… She knew that not all men would think the same way that Johnny had, but she really didn't want to get close to someone and lose her heart to him, only to find out that her infertility was a problem for him and he rejected her the same way that her husband had rejected her. Then again, how could you start any kind of relationship with someone by asking them if they wanted children? It just wasn't appropriate, not at that stage. So it was easier just to duck the issue and keep everyone on a friends-only basis, rather than risk getting involved with someone she'd end up disappointing.

Jamie hadn't actually replied to her text saying that she was on her way to meet him, and Anna felt slightly antsy as she headed towards the park. Would he be there? Or had he had time to think about it over the weekend and decide that he couldn't handle any part of Christmas, after all?

He owed her nothing. They barely knew each other. If he didn't turn up, it would be her own fault for trying to steamroller him into doing something he really didn't want to do.

But she hoped that he'd let her at least try to help him.

When she reached the entrance to the park and saw him leaning against the metal railings, her heart gave a little skip. Which was completely inappropriate. They were meeting this afternoon simply as colleagues who were in the early stages of friendship; it was a kind of quid pro quo thing. If she could help him, then he would help her. This wasn't a *date* date. Yes, he was gorgeous: tall and brooding, with those enormous cornflower-blue eyes, dark hair that she suspected would be outrageously curly if it wasn't so short, and a full, sensual mouth. But he wasn't dating her. Full stop.

Her heart gave another of those ridiculous little skips when Jamie saw her and lifted a hand in acknowledgement. Oh, for pity's sake. She needed to get a grip.

'Hey. Thanks for coming,' she said as she reached him.

He inclined his head. 'How was your day?' he asked.

'Full of babies with bronchiolitis. There's a whole bay reserved just for our RSV-positive patients, poor little loves,' she said. 'Though I feel even sorrier for the parents.'

'Because the babies can't tell them how they feel, and they're tired and not eating well, and the parents are feeling utterly helpless because they can't do anything to make their babies feel better,' he said.

'That,' she said before she could stop herself, 'sounds like personal experience.'

He wrinkled his nose. 'Observation. I did my paediatrics rotation at this time of year, and I remember what it was like.'

But she knew she'd asked something a bit too personal. She'd better switch the subject back to work. 'What made you become a surgeon?' she asked.

'I really enjoyed my surgical rotation,' he said. 'And I like working with children. Making a difference. How about you?'

'It was a toss-up between obstetrics and paediatrics,' she said. 'Helping to bring a new life into the world—that's so special and I loved every minute. And actually delivering a baby was so wonderful. But then I did my paediatrics rotation at Christmas, and that decided me. It's where I feel I can make the most difference, so that's why I chose the specialty.' She smiled at him. 'So. Shall we?' She gestured to the park.

Jamie really didn't want to do this.

But he'd had the best part of two days to come up with a reasonable excuse, and he hadn't found one. Plus, part of him wanted to be able to handle Christmas again without making his family miserable. For the last three years, he'd chosen to work over the festive season rather than join in with the family celebrations, and he used work as an excuse not to see them very often in between.

He felt guilty for not spending time with them; but whenever he was with them, it was always so obvious how much they were trying hard not to say the wrong thing. He knew they worried about him, but he found it suffocating when they wrapped him in cotton wool. Being in a family situation reminded him so much of what he'd lost, and Christmas magnified it to the point where it was too much to handle. He knew he needed to make the effort. Just... This was going to be painful. Like picking at a scab. Bit by bit.

Facing Christmas.

The time of year he dreaded.

His doubts must've shown on his face, because she said gently, 'Are you sure you want to do this?'

No. He wasn't sure at all.

She took his hand and squeezed it briefly. 'Look, we don't have to walk around the Winter Festival. We can, I dunno, go back to the high street and grab something to eat, or get a takeaway and go back to mine to chill out with some old comedies on TV—and then you can meet George.'

'George?' That got his attention. He was sure Anna had said she didn't have a partner. Or did she have a child? Was she a single mum? He hadn't heard any rumours on the ward, but then again he always closed his ears to gossip. 'Who's George?'

'George the Gorgeous Goldfish.'

He looked at her, not quite sure he'd heard that correctly. 'George is your *goldfish*?'

'Gorgeous goldfish,' she corrected. 'Yes.'

It was so incongruous that he couldn't help smiling. 'George the Gorgeous Goldfish,' he repeated.

'That's right. Obviously it's not quite like having a dog, because he doesn't stick his chin on my knee and look up at me with big brown adoring eyes, and he doesn't want to go for walks in the park or play ball. But I talk to him and he likes my singing.'

Singing to a goldfish.

That definitely wasn't what he'd expected to hear her say.

It was so surreal that he found himself smiling and walking into the park with her.

And then somehow they were right in the

middle of the Christmas fair, strolling up and down the path lined by little wooden pop-up shacks selling food, drink, Christmas decorations and every kind of gift you could think of, from candles to cosmetics to jewellery to hand-knitted Christmas jumpers. There were fairy lights draped over the roofs of the shacks, and garlands of greenery.

'I hope you're hungry,' she said, 'because I'm ravenous. I didn't get time for lunch.'

'It's four in the afternoon,' he pointed out.

'Which is too early for dinner, but I need a Christmas cookie and a hot chocolate right now to keep my blood sugar level.' She grinned at him. 'Which I admit is just a terrible excuse, because I love hot chocolate and cookies.' She found a hot drink stall, tucked her arm into his and queued up. 'This one's on me,' she said.

He accepted a coffee; she dithered about having extra cream on top of her hot chocolate, but then said, 'No, because I'll have another one later, laced with cream liqueur.'

Just how long did she intend to spend at the fair? he wondered, but didn't ask.

Next was a cookie in the shape of a star, studded with chips of butterscotch. 'Perfect,' she said after the first bite. 'You have to try this, Jamie.' She broke off one of the arms of the star and handed it to him.

He had no real choice but to eat it.

When was the last time he'd eaten something and really tasted it, instead of it being simply fuel? This was delicious: buttery and sugary, zinging along his tastebuds. 'It's good,' he said. 'Thank you.'

'And now—shopping,' she said. 'I need some stocking-fillers.'

'You're not buying your Secret Santa present for the ward, are you?' he asked.

'I've already got that,' she said. 'Though you might find something here.'

'But then you'll know whose name I drew when they unwrap it,' he pointed out.

'True,' she said. 'OK. We'll do this methodically. We'll go all the way along each row and back up again, and then I'll decide what I'm getting. I have four sisters-in-law.'

He blinked. 'You're one of five?'

'The middle one,' she said. 'Two older brothers, a younger brother and a younger sister. All married, and all with children.'

Was it his imagination, or did a shadow just cross her face? He knew she wasn't married and he was pretty sure she didn't have children. But was that by choice?

'And I got to be best woman at my sister Jojo's wedding to Becky,' she said with a smile. 'Which was so cool. How about you?'

'Youngest of three. Two older sisters,' he said. 'Both married with children.'

'Being an aunt,' she said, 'is fabulous, because I get pictures drawn for me all the time and there's always someone to play games with or read stories to or cuddle.' She smiled. 'We had the best family holiday ever, this summer—we all stayed at a villa in Tuscany, with Mum and Dad. And, even though we've got very different interests between us, we've also got enough in common to get on really well together. I know they always say the middle child is the peacemaker, but fortunately I don't have to be.'

He'd guessed right from when he'd first met Anna that she was part of a huge family; she had that confidence about her, that surety of being loved by everyone and being able to talk to anyone. She clearly adored her family, and it made Jamie feel guilty for pushing his away. He did love his parents and his sisters and his nieces and nephews; but he hated how everyone seemed to alternately tread on eggshells around him or try to jolly him into moving on. So he'd reasoned that it was easier for everyone if he tucked himself out of the way and buried himself in work, and the distance between them seemed to stretch more with every day.

'Uh-huh,' he said.

'So how old are your nieces and nephews?' she asked.

'Between six and ten,' he said. And now he felt even more guilty. Anna was clearly a very hands-on aunt. Just as Hestia had been; she'd always been happy to play games with Josh, Caitlin, Dylan and Layla, and she'd had a stock of books about ballerinas that she'd read to all four of them, saying that ballet wasn't just for girls. She'd even taught them all some steps, and the kids had loved putting on performances on family Sunday afternoons. She'd taken them to performances, too, and they'd all been spellbound by *The Nutcracker*. Especially when they'd seen their auntie Hestia dancing on the stage, pirouetting and leaping.

He'd been a hands-on uncle, too, back in those days. He'd read stories, built train tracks and done pretend tea parties with teddies. Hestia's death had meant that the children had lost their uncle as well as their aunt, and he felt bad about that. For their sakes, he should've made more of an effort.

He'd start with Christmas, he decided. *This* Christmas.

He'd let Anna help him face Christmas again and get his family back; and in turn he'd help her by playing Father Christmas for the ward. OK, so he wasn't ever going to get to the stage where he could open his heart to another partner, but he knew his family deserved much better than this. He needed to change. And he needed help to do it; on his own, he knew he'd just back away again because it was too hard to face.

'Mine are a little bit younger—Will's the oldest, at eight, and Ivy's the baby. Literally, because she's six months old next week,' Anna said. 'Mum and Dad managed to space us all two years apart, and it seems to be a tradition in my generation that you get to thirty and have a baby.'

Except for her? There was a definite shadow in her eyes now, Jamie thought, but it felt like prying to ask. He didn't want to hurt her, not when she was being so kind and sweet.

She gave him a super-bright smile. 'I've already bought and wrapped all their main presents so, as I said, I'm looking for stocking-fillers.'

'You've already bought and wrapped everything? But it's only November,' he said.

'It's December next weekend,' she corrected. 'Being organised means I get to find the perfect presents without any pressure and I also have the time to wrap them. My oldest brother refuses to go shopping until the day before Christmas Eve.' She rolled her eyes. 'That'd drive me bananas, dealing with the heaving crowds and risking having to rethink what I'm buying because what I want is out of stock.'

'So you're a planner?'

'Better believe it,' she said with a grin. 'I have spreadsheets, the lot. I keep a file of exactly what I've bought and for whom. It means I don't accidentally buy the same thing twice for one of my nieces and nephews—or buy the same book for one of the siblings, unless it's one that's been loved to bits and I'm replacing it.' She smiled. 'Perhaps you can help me look for something.'

Christmas shopping.

Hestia had loved Christmas shopping. She'd loved wrapping the presents, too, all ribbons and bows and garlands. Since her death, Jamie had bought mainly gift vouchers as presents; if he had bought an actual gift, he'd done it online and chosen the 'wrap it for me' option rather than doing it himself.

Now he realised how impersonal his actions must have seemed to his family, and he felt ashamed. They loved him and they missed Hestia, too. They'd all felt the loss of the little girl who hadn't had the chance to join them. He should've let them grieve with him instead of pushing them away.

'Perhaps you can help me, too,' he suggested.

She beamed. 'I'd love to. Buying presents is my favourite thing in the world. Right. Tell me all about your nieces and nephews.'

Uh... How did he admit that he didn't have a clue? That he'd let so much distance creep in between himself and his family that he didn't know what the kids were interested in any more? And children changed so much at their ages. 'Dylan's ten, Layla and Josh are eight, and Caitlin's six.'

'Are the girls super-girly? And do they have long hair or short?' she asked. 'Because hair ties and hair slides always go down well. Megan's six and anything heart-shaped or glittery gets pounced on with absolute glee.'

'Heart-shaped and glittery,' he said. That hadn't occurred to him. 'I think that would be good.'

'And art stuff. My nieces love paints and pens and notebooks. And books. I know they've got a fabulous bookstall here. Do Dylan and Josh like reading?'

'I think so,' he said carefully.

'Let me show you Will's favourite—he's the same age as your Josh. And the bookstall people might have a good idea for something suitable for Dylan,' she said.

Between them, they bought bangles and hair slides and scrunchies from the accessory stall, then moved on to look at the scented candles. Anna pounced on one for her mother. 'Look at this!' she said gleefully. 'Put a tealight in the middle, and the heat makes the carousel spin round with six filigree owls dangling down. My mum loves owls, so she'll *adore* this.'

He ended up with organic bath bombs and body butter for his mother and his sisters, ale from a microbrewery for his father and his brothers-in-law, books for all four nieces and nephews, a wooden duck with red Wellington boots for Caitlin, and a beautifully carved and painted wooden turtle for Layla, who he remembered loving the sea life centre when she was younger.

'What do you get an eight-year-old and a ten-year-old boy?' he asked.

'Once you get them off the games console?' she asked. 'I've already bought Will one of those mini planetarium projectors. I think I saw something similar on one of the stalls earlier.'

'I think Josh would like that, too,' he said.

'And I'm on the look-out for one of the magic science kits—the ones where you use all sorts of household objects to do tricks,' she said. 'Like adding vinegar to bicarb soda and a bit of food colouring to make lava.'

'I think that would go down well with Dylan,' Will said thoughtfully.

Once they'd finished their shopping, she looked at him. 'Wrapping paper?' she asked.

Jamie shook his head. 'I don't wrap.'

She grinned. 'Considering what you do for a living, you really can't get away with the excuse of not being neat enough.'

He couldn't help smiling back. 'There's a big difference between surgical stitching and wrapping awkward parcels.'

'Excuses, excuses, Mr Thurston,' she teased, and made him buy beautiful gift bags and tissue paper.

It was the first time in three years that he'd actually enjoyed something to do with Christmas. His family were all going to be in shock, he thought, when he handed over actual presents instead of the usual envelopes containing gift vouchers. But a good shock. And he might even brave going to see them after his shift on Christmas Day this year, instead of relying on his usual excuse of work. Thanks to Anna's advice, he was pretty sure that the kids were going to love the stocking-fillers he'd bought them.

Anna was prepared and had several foldable shopping bags in her handbag, a couple of which she lent to Jamie. The least he could do in return was offer to carry her purchases, too. And together they wandered through the fair.

There was a huge Ferris wheel at one end, all lit up, with people queueing for a ride.

'Do you want to go up on that?' she asked.

He nodded at their parcels. 'Probably not with this lot.'

But then he saw the carousel. Parents were lifting tiny children onto one of the carved wooden horses, and a fairground organ was playing Christmas songs and Christmas carols. Jamie could see the wonder on the little ones' faces as they went round and round on the horses. If life had happened the way it was supposed to, Giselle would've been nearly three and the perfect age for enjoying this.

He was coping with this. Just.

But then the song changed. To the one he couldn't avoid. 'All I Want for Christmas is You.' The song Hestia had loved so much. She'd even got her ballet class to do a special routine to it…

Cold stole through him, and it wasn't just the temperature outside now the sun had set. This was a bone-deep thing. The misery was back. Big time.

As if she noticed, she said softly, 'Time to find dinner. What would you like?'

'Anything.'

She bit her lip. 'Sorry. I've pushed you too far today, haven't I?'

'No. You've… It's helped,' he said. And it had, until he'd seen the carousel and heard that music, and loss had ripped through him again.

'When I feel low,' she said, 'I pick things that make me feel good. Decent food—not junk, something really nutritious—music, and some fresh air. Let's go get something to eat.'

Again, she hadn't pushed him to talk and she definitely wasn't prying. But the fact that she'd admitted she felt low at times made him realise that she understood how he was feeling right now. So he followed her away from the Ferris wheel and the carousel towards the food stalls.

'OK. Do you have any food allergies, and are you vegetarian?' she asked.

'No allergies, and I eat pretty much anything,' he said.

'All righty. We could have Christmas dinner in a burrito,' she said. 'Or a calzone with turkey, cranberry and cheese filling.'

'What would you prefer?' he asked, suddenly curious.

'My go-to comfort food is macaroni cheese,' she said. 'But I know it's not the best thing in the world, so I try to mix some greens and some veg in with it, to balance it out a bit.'

'I don't notice what I eat,' he admitted. Since Hestia's death, he'd seen food just as fuel and not as a pleasure.

'My best friend made me do mindfulness,' she said. 'I thought it was all hype, and I admit I've really mocked the stuff where you're supposed to eat a single raisin and take ages over it. It's so extreme. But there is a point to it. If you pay attention and notice things like colour and texture and scent, it does help to ground you a bit and it takes your mind off whatever's dragging you down. It's a kind of breathing space.' She shrugged. 'Plus I happen to know a stall here where they do really, *really* excellent macaroni cheese.'

'That,' he said, 'sounds good to me.'

'And I know this isn't the greatest nutrition, considering how I've just been banging on about healthy food,' she said, 'but last year there was a stall here that did churros covered in glitter sugar. Which I think would be perfect with a hot chocolate. And I am *so* planning to have that second one today.'

'These,' he said, 'are on me. Let's find a table.'

* * *

Anna sat thinking when Jamie left her with their shopping and queued up to get their food. That moment when he'd gone all brooding on her by the carousel, when they'd seen parents lifting their small children onto the horses, made her sure that whatever was hurting him was something to do with a child.

Yet every day he worked with sick children. How could he bear it, if it ripped his heart in two all the time?

They barely knew each other, and she knew she shouldn't push him to talk—especially because then he might start asking awkward questions of his own. Such as why she wasn't like the rest of her siblings, happily married and having children when she got to thirty.

On the other hand, talking to a stranger and getting a different perspective on things might help him.

Or maybe she should just stop being such an interfering busybody.

'Penny for them?' Jamie asked, coming to sit opposite her and sliding a cardboard tray of macaroni cheese with spinach, complete with a wooden fork, across the table to her.

'My thoughts aren't worth a penny,' she

said, not wanting to hurt him by being nosy. 'Thank you. This looks fabulous.' She took a mouthful. 'And it tastes even better.' She noticed that he'd chosen the same.

'This was a really good choice,' he said after the first mouthful.

'Though I'm buying us churros,' she said. 'And hot chocolate laced with that cream liqueur.'

'So do you come to the Christmas fair here every year?' he asked.

She nodded. 'And it's got bigger every year. Usually I do it as a girly thing, either with my best friend or my sister and sisters-in-law.' She smiled at him. 'So you could say you're an honorary girl today.'

'Hence the churros with glitter sugar,' he said dryly.

'Wait until you try them,' she said. 'I recommend the cinnamon glitter sugar. And I want to go back and get some of the Christmas candles. The ones that smell of orange and cinnamon and cloves—and they're for me, because I love candles at this time of year. Me, Gorgeous George, a good movie, some popcorn and a candle: that's a perfect night in.'

'Thank you,' he said. 'For pushing me into doing this.'

'So you're not hating every minute of it?' she checked.

'Not *every* minute,' he said. 'I've done my Christmas shopping and the food's good.'

'So what's the hardest thing about Christmas?' she asked before she could stop herself.

He was silent for so long that she thought he wasn't going to answer, and she was about to squeeze his hand and apologise for prying when he said quietly, 'The music. Certain songs. I...' He grimaced and shook his head.

'OK. So we'll try to avoid music for the future.' At least until he was more comfortable with other aspects of the holiday season. 'Can I ask—modern or carols?'

'Modern,' he said.

'I'll try to remember,' she said. 'I don't want to make this hard for you, Jamie. I want to help make things better.'

'You are,' he said. 'And seeing how much you love Christmas—I'm beginning to understand.'

'Just wait for the glitter churros,' she said.

Clearly he thought she'd been exaggerating to tease him, because when she came back from buying their hot chocolates and churros, she saw his beautiful cornflower-blue eyes widen. 'They really *are* glittery.'

'They started doing them last year. I'm on a mission to persuade the hospital canteen to start stocking them and I don't care if they're bad for your teeth—they're so lovely and up-lifting,' she said with a grin. She set the box between them, and their paper cups of hot chocolate on either side. 'Sorry. I forgot to ask if you wanted cream on top.'

'It's fine without,' he said.

And it was fine, until her fingers brushed against his while they were dipping the chur-ros into the pot of chocolate sauce. Her skin tingled where he touched her: which was ridic-ulous. They were colleagues, just about start-ing to become friends. She knew they both had baggage that would get in the way of any-thing else, so she really had to get a grip in-stead of letting herself give in to fantasies that just couldn't ever happen.

Or she could blame her feelings on the sugar rush of the churros.

Because nothing remotely romantic was going to happen between herself and Jamie Thurston.

She hauled herself back under control and made light conversation until they'd finished eating.

'Guess it's time to go home,' she said. 'George will be wondering where I am.'

'I hate to put a downer on you, but don't goldfish have a memory of about three seconds?' Jamie asked.

'Actually, no. My nephew Will did a summer project on goldfish last year. He spent ages researching on the Internet, and then he did a flashy presentation for me. Apparently, there's a university study where goldfish learned to press a lever to dispense food. The researchers changed it so the lever would only work for one certain hour a day, and the fish learned to press the lever during that one-hour window so they'd get the food. And in another study the researchers rang a bell at feeding time for a month, released the fish into the sea, then played the sound five months later and the fish came straight back, expecting their dinner.'

'Like Pavlov's dog—Pavlov's fish?' Jamie asked.

'Exactly. George knows my routine.' She

smiled. 'So I'd better make a move. Thanks for coming to the Christmas fair with me.'

'It wasn't as hard as I expected,' Jamie admitted.

'Good. So tomorrow you're going to give me your menu choices for the ward's Christmas meal,' she said. 'And are you free on Thursday evening?'

'Yes.'

'Maybe we can go skating on Thursday. Shall I book tickets for eight o'clock?'

He took a deep breath. 'OK. My aversion therapy for Christmas continues. Are you good at skating?'

'That's for me to know and you to find out,' she said, waggling her eyebrows at him.

'Better than bowling?'

She laughed. 'Don't be mean. Are you good at skating, then?'

'I'm taking the Fifth on that one.'

'You can't. You're not American,' she pointed out. 'Can you skate, or do I need to find out if they have an adult version of those penguins they use for toddlers?'

To her delight, he actually laughed. 'I am *not* going to a skating rink and holding on to a ginormous penguin.'

'Oh, good. So you *can* skate. I'll be expecting flashy moves, you know. Axle jumps, swizzles and twizzles, and camel spins.'

He looked at her. 'Did you just make those up?'

'Nope. I can assure you, they're all real moves.'

He looked horrified. 'So you're practically a professional skater.'

She took pity on him. 'More like I love watching that show when they have celebs learning to skate with the pros, and I've picked up all the lingo from there.' Then she frowned. 'Actually, that's a point. There's going to be music at any skating rink in London, and I promised you we'd avoid music. Would you rather we did something else?'

'Yes,' he said, 'but isn't the point of aversion therapy to face the thing that makes you uncomfortable?'

'It is,' she agreed, 'but I don't want to push you so far out of your comfort zone that you run back to the centre at the speed of light and never come out again.'

'We'll go skating,' he said.

'And if it gets too much for you, then we

can leave,' she said. 'Even if it's in the middle of a song.'

'That's a more than fair compromise. Thank you. I'll walk you home,' he said, and carried her parcels all the way back to her gate.

'You're very welcome to come in for a cup of coffee and to meet George,' she said.

'Another time, maybe,' he said. 'See you tomorrow.'

'See you.' And funny how his smile made her feel all warm inside.

CHAPTER FOUR

ON MONDAY EVENING Anna went straight from work to have dinner with her sister Jojo and sister-in-law Becky. She thoroughly enjoyed the chance to read a bedtime story to two-year-old Noah, even though part of her couldn't help thinking wistfully of what might have been. If her own plans had worked out, she would have done this every night with her own children, sharing stories and cuddles and laughter.

But she was lucky enough to see lots of her nephews and nieces and to share in their upbringing, so she wasn't going to let herself whine about what might have been.

Once she'd kissed her nephew goodnight and gone downstairs, Becky shooed her and Jojo into the living room, and Jojo put a glass of wine into her hand.

'Righty. Spill the beans,' Jojo said.

'I have absolutely no idea what you're talking about,' Anna said.

'*Interesting.* Because you went to the Christmas fair in the park yesterday,' Jojo said.

'How do you know?' Anna asked, surprised.

'Because Gemma at work went, too, and she saw you.' Jojo gave a dramatic pause. 'Eating churros with a very nice-looking man, so she told me.'

'Why didn't she come and say hello, then?' Anna asked.

'Because it was obvious that you were on a date, and she didn't want to interrupt you.'

Anna rolled her eyes. 'Oh, stop fishing. It wasn't a date.'

'What was it, then?'

'Jamie's a friend.'

Jojo scoffed. 'Just good friends?' she asked, making the quote marks with her fingers. 'We all know what that really means.'

'He's my colleague.'

'There's nothing wrong with dating a colleague,' Jojo said with a smile.

'This is ridiculous.' Anna frowned. 'If you must know, he's our new orthopod, the one who's covering Nalini's maternity leave. I'm

trying to talk him into being Father Christmas
for me on the ward—except at the moment
he's saying no because he hates Christmas.'

'Why does he hate Christmas?' Jojo asked.

'I don't know,' Anna admitted, 'but I can't
really ask him, because it'd be unkind to pry.'

'True. But, if you don't know what the problem is, then you might inadvertently stamp on
a sore spot,' Jojo pointed out.

'You have a point. I think it might be something to do with kids, because he went a bit
brooding on me when we were near the carousel,' Anna said thoughtfully. 'On the other
hand, he's an orthopaedic surgeon specialising
in children's medicine, so he's around children
all day. Maybe I was misreading it.'

'You'll have to find a tactful way to ask
him,' Jojo said.

Anna shrugged. 'He'll tell me when he's
ready.'

Jojo frowned. 'What I don't get is, if he
hates Christmas, then why would he go to a
Christmas fair with you?'

'Because we've come to an agreement. If
I can help him to feel that Christmas is bearable, then he'll wear the red suit and beard
and play Father Christmas on the ward for

me on Christmas Day, in Robert's absence,' Anna explained.

'So what do *you* get out of it?' Jojo asked.

'What it is to have a lawyer for a sister. I should've guessed you'd interrogate me,' Anna said lightly. 'I've already told you the deal. I'm helping Jamie to face Christmas, and then he'll help me by being Santa.'

'That's work,' Jojo pointed out. 'I mean, what do you personally get out of it?'

'Being Anna the Fixer?' Anna suggested.

'Not enough.' Jojo looked at her. 'If you're helping him get over his hatred of Christmas, then I reckon in return he needs to help you get over Johnny.'

'I'm already over Johnny,' Anna protested. 'So I don't need any help.'

'Yes, you do. You haven't dated anyone since your divorce,' Jojo said. 'Which suggests to me that either you're still in love with Johnny—'

'Absolutely not,' Anna cut in.

'—or,' Jojo continued, unfazed, 'that Johnny's left you feeling that you're not enough for anyone.'

Trust her sister to hit the nail right on the

head. Jojo was the most clear-sighted person she knew.

'And that isn't fair or true. You're wonderful, and any decent bloke would be lucky to have you. You need to get back out there and find someone who loves you for who you are. Someone who deserves you,' Jojo declared.

'I don't need anyone,' Anna said. 'Remember, I have Gorgeous George.'

'A goldfish,' Jojo said firmly, 'is not the same as having a partner.'

'Actually, George is better. He doesn't talk back to me and annoy me.' Anna gave Jojo a pointed look. 'Unlike interfering little sisters.'

Jojo hugged her. 'I'm not interfering, Anna-Banana. Really. I just worry that you're lonely.'

'How can I be lonely when I have the best family in the world and a ton of really good friends?' Anna asked.

'You come home to an empty house every night.'

Anna spread her hands. 'So do lots of people.'

'I think Johnny and his selfishness really chipped away at your self-confidence,' Jojo said. 'You don't bother dating anyone, because you don't believe a man will give you a second look as soon as they find out that you can't have children.'

Anna sighed. 'I'm fine, Jojo. Really. And I know not everyone shares Johnny's views about infertility. Not everyone even wants children in the first place.'

'I'm still not sure you've really come to terms with the situation yourself,' Jojo said gently.

'Honestly, I have,' Anna said. 'And you'd be the first person I'd talk to if I was upset about anything.'

Jojo still looked worried. 'I hope you know I'll always be here for you. And I hope you don't think Becky and I rub Noah in your face.'

'You don't. At all.' Anna was very definite about that. 'I love him. I love the fact you both asked me to be his godmother. And I love that you and Becky let me come and read him stories and play with him whenever I want to.'

'Because we love you, too.' Jojo still looked worried. 'So do you like this Jamie guy?'

'As a colleague and potentially a friend, yes.'

Jojo raised her eyebrows.

Anna sighed. 'All right. Yes, I admit he's

attractive. He reminds me of the actor in that Scottish historical drama everyone moons over.'

'*Nice*,' Jojo said approvingly. 'Does he like you?'

'I have absolutely no idea! I've only known the guy for a week. And this isn't about relationships, anyway. Though I suppose I should think myself lucky you didn't arrange for a suitable someone to partner me at dinner tonight,' Anna added ruefully.

'I wouldn't do that to you.'

It was Anna's turn to raise her eyebrows at her sister.

'Not without warning you first,' Jojo amended. 'But, if you like this Jamie guy, there's no reason not to make this Christmas deal of yours into a proper date.' She grinned. 'As he's a surgeon, at least you know he's going to be good with his hands.

'Joanna Maskell, you really are just too much, sometimes!' But Anna couldn't help laughing. 'Now, please can we drop the subject?'

To her relief, Jojo agreed; Becky called through that dinner was ready, and they kept the conversation light for the rest of the evening.

When Anna left, Jojo hugged her at the door. 'Sorry for nagging. I do love you, Anna, and I worry about you. So does Becky.'

'I'm fine. And I love you both, too. And Noah.' Anna hugged her back. 'See you soon.'

Anna didn't see Jamie on the ward and wasn't in clinic with him during the rest of the week, but on Thursday evening she met him at the Tube station as they'd arranged, and they went to the skating rink at Somerset House. There was a massive Christmas tree at either end of the skating rink, both of them covered in twinkling lights. Spotlights dappled the surface of the rink with different colours, and the rink was already packed with people, some looking nervous and sticking very close to the edge where they could grab the sides for safety, and others almost dancing on the ice. There was a pop-up Christmas shop selling gifts, and a stall selling hot drinks and snacks.

The music was all modern and Christmassy, and Anna could see that Jamie looked antsy; she remembered him telling her that he found Christmas music difficult.

'If you'd rather not do this, we don't have to,' she said.

Jamie looked awkward. 'But we're here now and you've already bought the tickets. It'd be a waste not to use them. Which reminds me, I still owe you the money for my ticket.'

'We'll sort that out later. Let's just go round the rink for one song,' she said. 'Then we can review the situation and see if it's too much or if you want to keep going for a bit longer.'

'OK.' He took her hand and squeezed it briefly. 'Thank you. You're being very patient with me.'

'I'm a doctor, not a patient,' she quipped lightly. 'And, for that matter, so are you.'

He groaned. 'That's terrible, but you know what I meant. I appreciate what you're doing for me.'

'You're doing just as much for me, actually. This means I have someone different to drag out to all the Christmassy things I love doing and my family and friends have had more than enough of,' she said with a smile. 'Plus I have my eye on the big prize.'

'What prize?' He looked mystified.

'You wearing that red suit on Christmas Day—because, apart from the fact that I haven't managed to source a voice-changer yet, what if it fell off while I was walking through the ward, or my beard fell off to reveal it? I really don't want to be responsible for making a whole ward of sick children find out the hard way that Father Christmas isn't real.'

And then she regretted it when he looked even more panicky.

'Sorry. I'm bulldozing you again. Ignore me. Let's skate.'

They queued up to hire skates, changed into them, and started to make their way round the rink.

'You're much better at skating than you are at bowling,' Jamie said to her.

She laughed. 'That's not exactly hard! But skating is just sliding one foot in front of the other. It's easier than having to aim for something and trying to hit it. And if you think I'm bad at bowling, you should see me at archery. Everyone dives for cover.' She rolled her eyes. 'So are you going to start doing all these spins and jumps and things?'

'Two letters. That's N and O, in exactly that order,' he said.

But at least he was smiling and starting to relax, she thought.

* * *

Skating on an ice rink.

Jamie hadn't done this in years. Hestia had always avoided skating, not wanting to risk slipping over on the ice and breaking an ankle; teaching ballet wasn't exactly something you could do easily while wearing a fracture boot. So he hadn't bothered either. But once he was used to the motion again, he found himself enjoying it.

Part of him was on edge, waiting for Hestia's favourite song to start playing and haunt him, but he forced himself to smile because he didn't want Anna to feel bad. She was trying so hard to help him, and he appreciated that she was trying to take the sting out of the festive season for him. And she clearly loved being out here on the rink, in the middle of the crowd among all the lights and with cheerful Christmas pop songs belting out.

All they needed now was for it to snow. Not the stuff that would settle and make all the pavements slippery enough to cause mayhem, but a few light, fluffy flakes that melted when they touched the ground, making the rink magical. And how weird was it that the idea actually appealed to him?

Then he realised that a child just in front of them was down on the ice, crying. He took Anna's hand and gestured over to the little boy. 'I think we should go and offer some help.'

She nodded, and they skated over.

'I'm Jamie and this is Anna. Can we help?' Jamie asked the little boy's mother.

She looked grateful. 'Thank you. I need to get him back on his feet before someone skates into him.'

Jamie helped her pick him up, but the little boy wouldn't stop crying. He was holding his arm, not letting anyone touch it. And Jamie had the strongest feeling he knew what had just happened.

'I'm a doctor,' he said gently. 'Can I have a look at your arm?'

The little boy shook his head.

'What's his name?' Anna asked.

'Adeoye—Ade for short,' the boy's mum said.

'Ade, does it hurt here?' Jamie asked, pointing to his own wrist.

Ade nodded, still sobbing.

'When you slipped over,' Jamie said, 'did

you put your hands down first to stop yourself falling flat on your face?'

Ade nodded, but this time he spoke, his voice almost hiccupping through the tears. 'It really hurts.'

Jamie could see that the boy's wrist was an odd shape and, given what Ade had just told him, he was pretty sure it was a Colles' fracture. 'Does it feel tingly or numb?

Ade shook his head.

That was a good sign. 'Do you feel dizzy or sick?'

'A bit,' Ade admitted.

'OK. That's probably the shock of falling.' Jamie turned to Ade's mother. 'I think he's broken his wrist—it's a special kind of fracture called a Colles' fracture.'

'It's really common when someone falls over onto an outstretched hand,' Anna said. 'We see a lot of them at the hospital when it's icy.'

'I can't do anything to help you here, because Ade will need an X-ray to check whether any of the bones need manipulating back into place before they put the cast on,' Jamie said. 'If you take him to the emergency department now, they'll do an X-ray and put a back slab on to keep his wrist stable overnight, then they'll probably put a lightweight cast on tomorrow morning.' He smiled at her. 'I'm an orthopaedic surgeon, for children, so I do a lot of this sort of thing.'

Ade's mother bit her lip. 'Will he be in a cast for long? He's got the school Christmas concert in a couple of weeks.'

'I'm sure they won't mind him being in a cast,' Anna said, 'and at least you'll have time to alter any costumes around the cast, if you need to.'

'If it's a straightforward fracture,' Jamie said, 'he'll have a cast on for four to six weeks, and then he'll need to do exercises every day to get his wrist properly mobile again.'

'I'd better get him to hospital,' she said.

'St Thomas' is the nearest emergency department to here,' Jamie said. 'I worked there for a bit. They're really nice. It's about ten minutes from here in a taxi and twenty on foot.'

Ade's mother looked at her son, who was still guarding his arm. 'I'll call a taxi now.'

'We'll help Ade with his skates while you make the call,' Anna said, 'and we'll wait with you until the taxi gets here.'

She was a natural with children, Jamie thought, telling the boy a stream of terrible jokes to distract him from the pain and even managing to make him laugh. Ade's mother thanked them when the taxi arrived, and then Anna looked at Jamie. 'Review time, then. Stop now, or have another skate?'

There was a hopeful look on her face, and he was pretty sure which one she'd choose. 'Another skate,' he said. 'And then I'm guessing it's hot chocolate?'

'That sounds utterly perfect,' she said, smiling at him.

And how crazy was it that his heart suddenly felt as if it had done a backflip?

This wasn't supposed to happen. It wasn't part of their deal. They were colleagues, sort of on the way to becoming temporary friends. They weren't supposed to get close and personal.

She was the first woman since Hestia to make him feel like that. Her warmth and her huge, huge heart just drew him. Yet, at the same time, he was pretty sure that Anna was hiding some deep sadness in her own past. She deserved more than he could give her. So he forced himself to keep things light.

Until the moment when she stumbled and he caught her so she didn't fall.

She looked up at him, those beautiful sea-green eyes wide and her lips very slightly parted.

And he knew then that it would be, oh, so easy to dip his head slightly. Brush his mouth against hers. Wrap his arms round her, and then deepen the kiss until they were both dizzy…

Was it his imagination, or was she staring at his lips, the way he was staring at hers? Did she feel the same thing? Did she want him to kiss her?

His tongue felt as if it had been glued to the roof of his mouth. He couldn't say anything, do anything but try to resist this insane urge to kiss her.

But if he didn't resist… What then? Would she kiss him back?

He could hardly breathe.

Could he?

Should he?

And then she said, 'Thank you for saving me.'

Her voice broke the spell and brought his common sense back into play. No. Of course he shouldn't kiss her. He needed to be sensible.

'You're welcome,' he said. 'More skating?'

At least if he had to concentrate on putting one foot in front of the other, he wouldn't be thinking about how it would feel to kiss her. How her skin would feel against his. How she was tall enough to be a perfect fit in his arms...

'More skating,' she said.

He didn't dare glance at her expression to find out if she looked relieved or disappointed. Kissing was absolutely not an option. This wasn't a date.

He just needed to concentrate on his footwork and the music. So far, he'd been lucky and they hadn't played That Song. Hopefully they'd already played it enough times earlier in the evening. Two more songs, and he'd suggest they get hot chocolate and leave.

Anna knew she was really making an idiot of herself. Fancy almost falling at Jamie's feet, like the poor little boy who'd slipped over earlier.

And then, when he'd grabbed her to steady her, it had felt as if she'd been galvanised.

Propinquity, that was what it was. Or maybe the bright lights dazzling her, the magical feel of the skating rink taking her out of the real world and letting her see the possibilities. Tempting her to do something that really wouldn't be sensible in real life.

For a moment, she'd found herself staring at his mouth and wondering what it would be like if he kissed her. How soft and teasing and inviting his mouth would be. How it would feel to have his arms wrapped round her, holding her close to him.

But that wasn't the deal.

She was supposed to be making him feel better about Christmas, showing him the good side of the season and taking the sting out of whatever had hurt him in the past, not flinging herself at the poor man and embarrassing both of them. He'd made it perfectly clear that he wasn't in the market for a relationship, and neither was she. She needed to focus on skating. Skating, not kissing. She repeated the mantra to herself half a dozen times, hoping that somehow it would stick in her head. Skating, not kissing. Skating, not kissing…

But all the time she found herself very aware of him. The space he took up. His height. His dark good looks, those gorgeous cornflower-blue eyes, that shy and so-rare smile.

Get a grip, Anna, she told herself crossly. This isn't a date. Stop thinking about the what-ifs, because there aren't any.

Two more songs and they'd leave.

They went round and round the skating rink, and she couldn't help noticing how the other couples there were skating hand in hand, how the more confident ones stopped and spun their partner round into their arms and kissed them despite no mistletoe being in evidence.

She wasn't meant to be noticing the kissing.

Concentrate on the skating, she told herself fiercely. Even if it was driving her slightly crazy.

Maybe she needed some hot chocolate, a sugar rush to stop her thinking about the sweetness of his mouth. So, when the second song ended, she said, 'I'm done. Time for hot chocolate, I think.'

'Great idea,' he said.

Except, when they were in the queue, some-one bumped into them and Jamie ended up with his arms around her to protect her.

And all of a sudden there wasn't enough air. Despite the fact that they were outside and had the whole of London around them, there just wasn't enough air to suck into her lungs.

She made the mistake of looking into his eyes, and it looked as if it was the same for him because his pupils were absolutely enormous.

It isn't because of you, she told herself sharply. It's a physiological reaction to a low light area, that's all.

Except the lights weren't really that low. It was actually really, really bright in the courtyard, so anatomically speaking his pupils should be tiny.

The fact that they weren't made her heart skip a beat.

Was he going to kiss her?

On the skating rink, it would've been much too dangerous. Too easy for either or both of them to slip and fall. But here—here, they were on solid, unslippery ground.

Except it felt way more slippery than the rink.

If he kissed her, and she kissed him back… What then?

Right at that moment, she couldn't move. They were in the queue, pressed together, with his arms around her and his face really close to hers. Had she been five inches shorter, it wouldn't have been an issue. But their lips were well within kissing distance, and Anna really didn't know what to do.

It was the first time she'd actually wanted to kiss anyone since Johnny.

And, OK, she knew that kissing didn't necessarily *mean* anything. But she had a nasty feeling that, if she let him, Jamie Thurston could steal her heart. And she dared not risk that. It had taken her too long to put herself back together after Johnny. She wasn't looking for another relationship. Not even a temporary fling. Anna Maskell wasn't a fling kind of girl.

How could she move out of his arms without making a fuss and embarrassing both of them? Worse still, would he guess that she was moving away from him precisely because she wanted him to kiss her and this whole thing was driving her crazy?

She was saved by the waitress at the hatch asking, 'What can I get you?'

The people in front of them took their own drinks from the counter and left, giving her space to move away from Jamie, and he said, 'Two hot chocolates, please.' He sounded cool and calm, not as if they'd been seconds away from kissing each other dizzy *in public*.

The space helped, but it wasn't quite enough to stop Anna feeling like a teenager standing next to her crush at a high school disco. And she wasn't wearing ice skates any more, so she couldn't use her *skating, not kissing* mantra.

Somehow she managed to make light, fluffy conversation about skating and Christmas trees and decorations while they sat on one of the benches and drank their hot chocolate and watched the skaters, and then they headed back to Muswell Hill. The tube was too noisy for them to talk, giving her time to think, and on the way home Anna came to a decision. She knew how to neutralise the attraction now: she'd treat him in exactly the same way that she did her other male friends, so at the station she'd kiss him on the cheek, smile and say goodbye.

Except then Jamie offered to walk her home. She thought it would be a bit churlish to refuse, given that they were going the same way.

At her garden gate, she took a deep breath. Polite, she reminded herself. Pretend he's just like any other male colleague. 'You're very welcome to come in for a coffee or a glass of wine or something.'

Something? Oh, no. Please don't let him interpret that as her being like a teenager and talking in code for 'come in and snog me witless'.

To her relief—mingled with disappointment, if she was honest with herself—he said, 'Thanks, but I'd better be going.'

'OK. Thanks for coming skating tonight.' She paused. 'I hope it wasn't too difficult.' This whole thing was meant to be about helping him, not about her making a fool of herself and starting to want things she couldn't have.

'No. It was fun.' He looked surprised, as if he hadn't expected to enjoy it. 'Thank you for organising it.'

'No problem. See you at work tomorrow.' She stepped forward, intending to kiss him on the cheek; but somehow everything got a bit tangled and she ended up kissing him on the mouth instead. And her lips tingled, every nerve-end reacting to the touch of his skin.

Anna Maskell had a huge heart. She was warm and affectionate, the sort of person who kissed everyone, and it didn't mean anything, Jamie reminded himself.

Except he'd messed it up and, instead of kissing him on the cheek the way she'd obviously intended to, she'd kissed his mouth. And it was as if someone had just lit touchpaper and blown up some of the walls he'd built over the last three years, letting him *feel* again.

Dared he let himself want this? Dared he risk his heart with Anna?

They said that lightning didn't strike twice in the same place...

Which was an unfortunate metaphor, given what had happened to Hestia. Eclampsia, from the Greek for 'light burst'.

No. He couldn't do this. He couldn't offer Anna an uncomplicated relationship. So he needed to back off.

Now.

Before either of them got hurt.

'See you at work tomorrow,' he muttered, and left without looking back.

CHAPTER FIVE

'THE WAY I feel right now, anyone would think I was fourteen, not thirty-four,' Anna told George, dropping a blanched pea with the skin taken off into his tank. 'A fourteen-year-old who's just snogged a boy outside the school disco—the one she's secretly fancied for months—except it was really embarrassing instead of romantic because their braces clashed, and now she thinks he's going to tell his mates and everyone's going to laugh at her at school tomorrow.'

George swam up and ate the pea.

'Except obviously neither of us was actually wearing a dental brace. I know Jamie's not going to say anything at work, and neither am I. And I don't fancy him.'

George waggled his tail, as if to say, *Who are you trying to kid?*

'But it's just as embarrassing as a fourteen-year-old's brace-clash. There was me, thinking I could be all cool and calm and just kiss him on the cheek and treat him in exactly the same way that I treat every male in my life, and what do I do? I go straight in and kiss him on the mouth. How stupid am I?' She dropped a small piece of blanched broccoli into the tank. 'Eat your greens, Georgie-boy, because they're good for you.'

The goldfish did her bidding.

'Just as well it happened after I asked him in for a drink and he said no. Otherwise... Oh, for pity's sake.' She gave George another pea. 'Right, that's the end of your treats for today. I don't want to overfeed you and give you swim bladder.' She sighed and put the box of goldfish treats back in the fridge. 'I'm such an idiot,' she told the fish when she came back. 'I haven't dated anyone since Johnny, and I don't need to. I'm quite happy with my life as it is, and coming home to just you. But when I nearly fell over and Jamie caught me... We were quite close to kissing, right in the middle of the skating rink. He was definitely looking at my mouth.'

She plugged her phone into her speaker dock. 'I was just as bad. I did all that staring-at-the-mouth thing right back at him, and I actually wanted him to kiss me. And now I feel such a fool, and I hope I haven't wrecked our working relationship.' She grimaced. 'I'll just have to apologise to him tomorrow, tell him I don't know what on earth came over me, and explain that I'm really not looking for a relationship and he'll be perfectly safe with me in future. And I hope he'll still let me teach him about the magic of Christmas, or I really am going to have to practise a deep, booming voice and wear the red suit and beard myself. I hate to think I might be letting the kids down.'

George swam up and down his tank, as if in sympathy.

'Righty. There's only one way to get rid of feeling stupid and miserable,' she said, hit 'play', and started singing and dancing along to her favourite Wham! songs.

On Friday morning, she walked into work, wondering just how she was going to face Jamie on the ward. Maybe he'd be in Theatre today. Or maybe she'd get some good ideas after a cup of coffee.

But when she checked her clinic list, she knew she wasn't going to get away with it.

Eleven-year-old Lily Brown had been one of Nalini's favourite patients, and she was a favourite with Anna, too. Lily had scoliosis, and they'd worked with her for years, first with a plaster cast to help straighten her spine and then with a brace.

Now Lily was facing surgery, because despite the brace the curve in her spine was getting worse. She'd had the MRI scan last week, and a pre-op assessment a couple of days before to check her blood pressure and her pulse, and an ECG to check that her heart was fine. There weren't any contra-indications, so surgery looked like the best option.

Just as Anna was working through her checklist, there was a knock on her open door. She glanced up to see Jamie standing there.

In a suit rather than scrubs, he looked absolutely delicious.

And that was the most inappropriate thought she'd had all morning. It had to stop. Now. Because they were absolutely not getting together.

'Hi,' he said. 'I see you already have coffee. I was going to offer to make you one.'

'Thanks, but I'm fine.'

'I was wondering if we could have a chat

about Lily Brown before her appointment,' he said, 'and if you can get me up to speed. I saw from the notes that you've been working with her for years.'

And, just like that, it was easy again. They could focus on work. On their patient. They could ignore anything personal between them and simply concentrate on making a difference to the people who really mattered. She could almost have kissed him—if it wasn't for the fact that a kiss had caused all the awkwardness between them in the first place.

'Sure,' she said. 'Go grab yourself a coffee and I'll meet you in the consulting room with her scans.'

By the time she'd finished getting him up to speed with Lily's case, it was time to start clinic and she called Lily and her mother in.

'Lily, Heather,' she said, 'this is Mr Thurston, who's covering Nalini's maternity leave and is going to do the operation next week.'

'I'm Jamie,' he said, shaking their hands in turn. 'It's good to meet you, Lily and Mrs Brown.'

'Call me Heather,' Lily's mum said. 'We're practically permanent fixtures here and I prefer first names.'

'Heather,' Jamie said with a smile. 'OK. I've reviewed your MRI scan, Lily, from the base of your brain to the bottom of your spine, and there aren't any other problems we need to worry about. The special X-rays you had taken last week have shown me the flexibility of your spine and where I need to operate, and you passed your pre-op assessment with flying colours.'

Lily bit her lip. 'I wish Santa really existed,' she said, 'and that he'd bring me a new back so I didn't have to have an operation and make Mum worry so much about me.'

'This is the next best thing to a new back,' Jamie said, 'and I've done this operation a few times now, so I promise your mum doesn't have to worry. The team here is great, so you'll be in safe hands.'

'Is it going to hurt?' Lily asked.

'You'll be asleep while I operate, so you definitely won't feel any pain then,' Jamie said. 'Has anyone talked you through exactly what's going to happen?'

Lily shook her head.

'OK. I'll talk you through it, and then if there's anything I haven't covered you can ask me. On Sunday night, you'll come in to the hospital and stay here overnight. I'm afraid you won't be able to have anything to eat after about seven o'clock, which means no break-fast on Monday. Then you'll come to Theatre and I'll be there to meet you,' he said. 'We'll give you a pre-med to make you sleepy, put some special cream on the back of your hand so you won't feel the needle going in for the anaesthetic, and then we'll give you the an-aesthetic so you won't be awake during the surgery. And there will be a whole team of us looking after you in Theatre.'

He ticked off the team roles on his fingers. 'There will be the anaesthetist, who makes sure you stay asleep; the radiographer, who takes X-rays of your spine while you're asleep; a neurologist, who will be looking after your spinal cord during the surgery; and a team of nurses and another surgeon to help me.'

Lily looked thoughtful. 'Will you be there, Anna?'

'No, I'll be on the ward,' Anna said, 'but I'll come to see you afterwards.'

'Though Anna is very welcome to come into Theatre to see what I'm doing, if she has time between seeing her other patients,' Jamie said. 'The operation I'm going to do is something called a spinal fusion.' He took the model of a spine from the corner of the room. 'You probably already know these bones here are called vertebrae. I'm going to put wires and screws into your vertebrae and connect them to a rod so the curved bones will grow straighter, and then I'll put a bone graft over the wires and screws. Over the next year, the bone graft will grow with the existing bone in your spine and your spine will be straighter.'

Lily nodded.

'Is there anything you'd like to know?' he asked.

'Will it hurt?'

'You'll feel a bit sore after the surgery,' he said, 'but in a few months' time your back won't hurt as much as it does now. Yes, you will still get back pain every so often, but it won't be anywhere near as bad as it is now, and everyone gets a bit of back pain from time to time.'

'And I'll get taller?'

'You'll get taller,' he confirmed. 'Actually, you'll get taller during the operation. If you get your mum to measure you on the day of the op and mark it on your bedroom door-frame, then do the same when you're back home after the op, you'll be able to see exactly how much difference it's made.'

'And my back will be straight?'

'Straighter,' he said. 'You'll still have a little bit of a curve, but it'll be much less noticeable.'

'What happens after the surgery?' Heather asked.

'The anaesthetist will wake Lily up,' he said, 'and then you can see her. She'll go to the High Dependency Unit for a day or so, but then we can move her to the ward.' He smiled at Lily. 'You might feel a bit sick after the anaesthetic, but it will pass. And we'll give you painkillers so you won't be too sore.'

'How long will I have to stay in hospital?' Lily asked.

'Probably for about a week after your surgery,' he said. 'You'll gradually get more mobile. Walk a little bit every day and listen to what your physio says, because keeping moving will help you recover better. You'll be back at school probably about six weeks after your surgery.'

'So I'm not going to miss much?'

'No. And your friends can visit you on the ward, if you want.'

'It's a good idea to have a rota,' Anna said, 'so you get lots of people coming in to see you. And definitely have music and your phone, so you've got something to do. Having a headphone splitter would be good, because then you and your friends can listen to the same thing.

'We'll get one over the weekend,' Heather said. 'Is there anything else?'

'Pyjamas that button up the front, because they're easier to get on after the operation,' Anna said. 'Loose tops are best because they'll be more comfortable on the dressing. And you might find your lips and your face get a bit dry, Lily, so bring some moisturiser and lip balm.' She smiled. 'Your hair is lovely, but you might find it gets knotty, so I'd recommend having it in a plait rather than a ponytail or a bun.'

'And make sure you drink lots of fluids,' Jamie added. 'You might find in the first couple of days that light foods are easier to deal with—things like jelly, custard and yoghurts.'

'Pineapple,' Lily said with a smile. 'I love pineapple.'

'Me, too,' Jamie said. 'Does that answer all your questions, Lily, or is there anything else?

And nothing's too small or too silly. You can ask me whatever you like. I want you to feel comfortable coming in for the operation.'

Lily thought about it. 'No. Though I'm a bit scared.' She looked at her mother. 'In case I don't wake up.'

'You'll wake up,' Jamie reassured her. 'There are support groups. Maybe you can go onto one of the forums and talk to the people there; you'll meet lots of people who had the same operation at your age. They can tell you all sorts of tips and what it feels like after the operation, so it won't be so scary for you.' He quickly looked something up on the Internet, scribbled the website address down on a page of a reporter's notebook, then tore off the page and gave it to her. 'This is a good place to start. I'll see you on Monday morning, then, and if you've got anything else you're worrying about, just tell me.'

The rest of the clinic flew by, and then it was time for their break.

'Want to join me for lunch?' Jamie asked.

As colleagues? She could do that. 'Thanks. That'd be good.'

They headed for the canteen, bought lunch and found a quiet table.

'You were really good with Lily this morning, especially with those practical suggestions. I wouldn't have thought of them.'

She shrugged. 'You're a surgeon, and I work on the ward. I know what the aftercare's like, that's all. In my shoes you'd do the same.'

'But I saw your face in that consultation. Her case has really got to you, hasn't it?'

She nodded. 'That bit where she said she wished Father Christmas would bring her a new back for Christmas. I really wish I had a magic wand, sometimes, so I could really fix things.'

'We do the best we can,' Jamie said quietly. 'And that's the key thing. We do make a difference, Anna.'

'I know.' And she needed to finish clearing the air between them. 'Jamie, I want to apologise for last night.'

'No apology necessary.'

She rather thought he was just being nice. 'I want us to be able to work together, so I need to be honest with you. I'm not looking for a relationship. Last night, I think all the romance of the skating rink got to me—the tree, the lights and the music.'

'Uh-huh.' He didn't look convinced.

And now for the rest of it. 'I'm going to tell

you something now, but I want you to promise me first that you're not going to pity me.'

That got his attention. He looked straight at her. 'I promise, but you don't have to tell me anything.'

'No, I need to explain why I'm sticking just to friendships with people in future.' She swallowed hard. 'You know I said everyone in my family seems to hit thirty and have a baby?'

He nodded.

'That was the plan for me, too. My biological clock was ticking madly when I was twenty-eight, and over the next year my husband and I agreed I'd stop taking the Pill. The idea was that we'd wait three months to clear all the drugs from my system, then start trying for a baby.' And that was the sticky bit.

'Except my periods didn't actually come back. I did a couple of pregnancy tests, in case we'd slipped up and I was actually already pregnant—that happened to one of my friends—but the tests were all negative.' The disappointment had almost choked her. 'And then, when my period still didn't turn up, I started to wonder if something might be wrong with me. I spent a fortune on ovulation kits to see if my periods were just so superlight that I wasn't noticing them, but the tests all said I wasn't even ovulating.

'That's when I went to see my doctor, and he suggested we start by testing levels of my follicle-stimulating hormone. You're supposed to do the test on the fourth day of your cycle but, because we hadn't got a clue when my cycle actually was, he suggested doing a couple of tests six weeks apart. They both showed raised levels of FSH, and that confirmed that my ovaries had stopped working. My doctor diagnosed premature ovarian insufficiency. Fortunately I didn't have any of the other symptoms of menopause—no hot flushes, no mood swings, no night sweats—but the only way I was going to have a baby was with IVF and a donor egg. Which my husband didn't want to do.'

Jamie frowned. 'He didn't want to consider adoption or fostering?'

'He wanted an uncomplicated, very average pregnancy with a baby at the end of it. Which I couldn't give him. So he found someone who could.' She shrugged. 'It would've been nice if he'd ended our marriage first, but there you go.'

Jamie blinked. 'Your husband had an affair?'

'Yes. He knew he'd behaved badly, and that kind of made him worse—he was trying to justify himself.' She grimaced. 'And he did that by making me feel that no reasonable man would ever want to be with me because I wasn't able to have kids.'

'That's horrible, and it's also untrue.'

'I know, but it did mess with my head a bit for a while,' she admitted. 'But I've come to terms with it, now. And I'm really lucky. I have six nieces and nephews, and I've got a feeling that Jojo and Becky are getting broody again now that Noah's turned two. So there are lots of children in my life and I'm very happy to be a hands-on aunt. My brothers and sister all include me in family days out, and so do my friends, so I get to do all the things I would've done with my own kids. I just don't get all the broken nights and the tantrums and the super-evil nappies to go with them, and I won't get all the teenage angst and slammed doors and being told that I've ruined someone's life.' She smiled. 'There has to be an upside, right?'

Jamie rather thought that smile was forced; he could see there was still a kernel of hurt in her eyes. But now he understood what made her tick.

'Thank you for being so honest with me.'

'I just wanted you to know why I'm really not looking for a relationship. I've come to terms with my condition and I'm fine about it.'

'Your ex is a piece of...' He bit the words back.

'Yeah. His photograph ended up on a dartboard or two,' she said, 'and my brothers and my sister all wanted to go and punch him.'

'I think I want to punch him, too, right now.'

She shook her head. 'Violence doesn't solve anything. He was as hurt as I was by the situation, but he just didn't deal with it very well.'

'Which makes you a very noble person for not hating him for what he did.'

'I'm not that noble—I'm the one who put his photo on the dartboard,' she said. 'But actually I do feel a bit sorry for him. He really wanted a baby, and I think he kind of rushed into that relationship. They're not together any more and his ex is being a bit awkward about letting him see his daughter.'

Jamie stared at her in surprise. 'What? He told you all about that and expected you to be sympathetic?'

'No, his mum told me.' She smiled. 'I know there's this stereotype of the awful, interfering mother-in-law, but Maggie's lovely and we always got on really well. We stayed friends after the divorce and we have a catch-up lunch every so often. We just tend to avoid the subject of her son. I mean, it's not her fault that Johnny turned into a selfish toad. She didn't bring him up to be that way and she was so angry with him for the way he treated me. And the only reason I know about his situation now is because he's been living back with his parents since his ex dumped him. His mum had to rearrange one of our lunch dates so we could avoid me having to see him, and that's when it all came out.'

He thought about it. Despite the pain her ex had caused her, Anna had stayed in touch with his family. Whereas Jamie barely saw Hestia's parents or her sister, thinking it would be too painful for all of them; he would simply be a physical reminder of their loss. If Anna hadn't married him and fallen pregnant with Giselle, she wouldn't have had eclampsia, wouldn't have had that fatal haemorrhage, and she'd still be alive. But now, hearing Anna talk about her former in-laws, he could see a different side. Maybe they were lonely. Maybe seeing him would've given them a chance to talk about their daughter and sister, keep her alive in their heads. Guilt flooded through him. He should have made more effort with them; and he definitely shouldn't have shut his own family out.

'You're an amazing woman, Anna Maskell,' he said. 'It's impressive that you can have such a positive attitude towards something so painful and difficult.'

She shrugged. 'It isn't all me. I had counselling, and my counsellor showed me that all the "why me" pity-party stuff isn't at all helpful. She taught me to spin it round and think, "someone has to have this happen to them, so why *not* me?"'

Jamie didn't have an answer to that. He'd done the 'why me' himself so many times. And he'd refused counselling, despite being offered it. Maybe that had been a mistake. Maybe that was something he needed to do to move on. Or maybe not—because Anna was really helping him see a different side to things.

'So are you on any treatment?' he asked. Then he grimaced. 'Sorry. That's intrusive. Ignore it. I was being nosy and rude. You don't have to answer.'

'No, I'm fine talking about it, and actually that's one of the reasons I don't hide it away. I'm not the only woman in the world who's gone through a super-early menopause, and maybe I can pay things forward a bit and help someone who's struggling to deal with a similar situation, the way other people have helped me. Obviously at thirty-four I'm a couple of decades younger than most women with the menopause.' She smiled at him. 'So, yes, I'm having treatment. I'm on hormone replacement therapy to help keep up my bone density and avoid the risks of cardiovascular disease.'

'But doesn't HRT...?' He stopped.

'Put me at higher risk of breast cancer? No, actually, because of my age. It's fine. I need to be careful with my calcium intake, which is why I drink hot chocolate rather than tea and I take my coffee very milky, and I do a five-kilometre run twice a week because it's good weight-bearing exercise and helps with bone density. I have a DEXA scan every year to keep an eye on my bone density. So, as far as I'm concerned, everyone's looking after me. And I'm not letting my premature menopause or my infertility define me.'

'You're the sort of person who makes lemonade when life gives you lemons.'

'No—I make lemon drizzle cake and lemon meringue pie, actually. They're much nicer and slightly better for my teeth,' she said with a grin, making him laugh.

Even though she made him feel so light of spirit, at the same time Jamie felt guilty. Anna had been through a lot and she'd pushed herself to move on, whereas he was still wallowing in what had happened to him.

Then again, she was helping him move on now. Maybe he should tell her about Hestia and Giselle, explain why he found Christmas so hard. He opened his mouth to start that conversation, but the words stuck in his throat and refused to come out.

'So, anyway, now you know that you're totally safe with me,' she said. 'We can be friends.'

'Friends,' he agreed.

'And I hope you'll continue our Christmas bargain, because I really do want you as our ward's Father Christmas.'

'OK,' he said. 'What do you suggest next?'

'Maybe we could try a Christmas movie,' she said.

'That's fine. When?'

He was half expecting her to suggest watching a DVD at either his place or hers, but then she said, 'There's a special screening at the Alexandra Palace theatre on Monday night. First come, first served for seating, so if we get there early enough we'll get a decent seat. We could maybe go and get a pizza somewhere first.'

'Sounds good,' he said. 'OK. Let me buy the tickets.'

'How about I buy the tickets and you buy the pizza?' she suggested.

'That works for me,' he said. 'Thank you. Monday night it is. And it'll be a good way to decompress after Lily's surgery. I meant what I said earlier, by the way. If you want to observe any part of the operation, you're very welcome—as is anyone on our team who might find it useful.'

'I might just take you up on that.'

Weird how her sea-green eyes made his heart skip a beat. But, after what she'd just told him, Jamie knew how inappropriate the reaction was. Anna had made it very clear that she wasn't interested in anything more than friendship. So he'd stuff the feelings back inside rather than let them out to bloom.

CHAPTER SIX

ON MONDAY MORNING Jamie met Lily Brown outside the operating theatre.

'All ready?' he asked.

'I think so.' She gave him a nervous smile.

'Good.' He smiled at her; he noticed that her mother looked just as nervous, and patted Heather's arm. 'She'll be fine. I'm going to take my time over this so I get it right and Lily gets the best possible outcome.'

Heather nodded. 'I know. I just…'

He knew what she wasn't saying. 'Of course you're going to worry. You're her mum. Have you got someone who can wait with you during the op?'

'My friend's coming as soon as she's dropped her daughter off at school,' Heather said.

'Great. You can stay with Lily while she's having the anaesthetic, until she goes to sleep, but then I'm afraid we'll have to send you out for a cup of tea.' He smiled at her again. 'I'm going to go and scrub in—which means washing my hands super-thoroughly—and I'll see you on the other side, OK?' He turned to Lily. 'And I'll see you in Theatre, Miss Brown.'

The operating theatre was just how he liked it: quiet, with a Bach piano piece playing softly. He'd already managed to establish a good working relationship with his team, and thankfully they were happy with his choice of music to operate to.

'Good morning, everyone. I'll just run through what we're doing this morning and make sure everyone's happy with their roles,' he said.

Once that was done, he settled down to make the first incision and to make a huge difference to Lily Brown's spinal column.

Anna knew that Lily's operation was complex and would take at least four hours. She managed to get enough time to go and observe the operation during her lunch break, and saw for herself that despite the gentle teasing of her sister Jamie Thurston *was* really good with his hands.

He was also really nice with the rest of the team, just like Nalini was, treating everyone as a valued colleague; it was the total opposite of the arrogant surgeons who had been around when Anna had been a student. They'd viewed themselves as superior beings and considered any questions to be a personal attack on their abilities. She noticed that Jamie explained exactly what he was doing as he went along and why he'd chosen to use one particular method over another, and he was clearly happy to use any questions as a teaching point.

She really hoped that he'd agree to stay at Muswell Hill Memorial Hospital for a bit longer than his scheduled three months and cover the rest of Nalini's maternity leave, because he was a real asset to the team. And also, if she was honest with herself, because she liked him being around—even though she knew it was ridiculous and there was absolutely no possibility of a relationship between them. She was doing just fine on her own, and Jamie clearly wasn't ready to move on from whatever had broken his heart.

She lingered in Theatre for as long as she could, enjoying watching the procedure, then headed back to her clinic.

At the end of the day, she popped into the High Dependency Unit to see Lily. 'How are you doing?' she asked.

'OK.' But Lily's lower lip was wobbly, she noticed.

'I brought you something,' she said, and handed over a tube of lip salve. 'Just in case you forgot yours or you might like a different flavour for a change. This one's cocoa butter and it's really nice.'

'That's so kind of you.' Lily started to cry and scrubbed the tears away with the back of her hand. 'Sorry. I don't know why I'm crying. I should be happy because my back is going to be better and that means they're going to stop calling me Quasimodo at school.'

'You, honey, are an Esmeralda if ever I saw one, not Quasimodo,' Anna said, sitting on the side of her bed and exchanging a glance with Heather that told her Lily's mother had had no idea how bad the teasing had been and was horrified to learn what had been said to her daughter. 'You've been worrying about the operation and now it's all over and you're filled with relief, so that's probably why you're feeling a bit weepy—plus sometimes people react like that to the anaesthetic. It's absolutely fine and it's perfectly normal, so you don't need to apologise. The good news is that after a night's sleep you'll feel an awful lot better.'

Lily didn't look convinced, and Anna hated to think how terrible the poor girl had been feeling at school. But maybe there was something she could do to help. 'Actually, there are a lot of really kick-ass people with scoliosis. You know Usain Bolt?'

'No way,' Lily said, her eyes widening in surprise. 'But he's a famous sprinter.'

'Yup. The fastest man in the world has scoliosis—and it hasn't stopped him, has it?'

'That's incredible,' Heather said. 'I had no idea either.'

Anna went on to list half a dozen actresses and singers who had scoliosis—some of the most famous and beautiful people in the business, all of whom she hoped Lily might have looked up to.

'And they all have scoliosis?' Lily asked. 'Really?'

'Really,' Anna confirmed. 'Not all of them needed an op—some had a brace like the one you used to wear and that worked for them. But they all have scoliosis. So, next time anyone says anything horrible to you, just tell them those names. Show them that scoliosis is simply one part of you and it doesn't define you. You're awesome, Lily Brown, and don't let anyone ever tell you otherwise.'

'Anna's absolutely right,' Jamie said from the doorway. 'Though I didn't know that about Usain Bolt.'

'You do now,' Anna said with a smile. 'He's a great ambassador for the condition. And Princess Eugenie. She was a year older than you are when she was diagnosed, Lily.'

Lily nodded. 'I remember seeing the pictures in the paper. Her wedding dress was low at the back so you could see her scar. I thought she was so brave.'

'So are you. It's who you are inside that counts, and how you deal with life,' Anna said.

Who you are inside... How you deal with life.

And Anna herself was brave, Jamie thought. She had no scars on the outside to show how her life had been turned upside down by a medical diagnosis, but there were definitely scars on the inside. Yet she carried on and made the best of things. He rather thought he could learn a lot from her.

More visitors arrived to see Lily, and Anna smiled. 'We'll go now and let you catch up with everyone. I'll see you on the ward tomorrow.'

'Yes, and I want to see you on your feet—even if it's only for two steps,' Jamie said. 'You're doing brilliantly. It's good to see you smiling.'

'Thank you. Thank you so much for everything you did for me,' Lily said.

'Pleasure. That's why I do this job—so I can make people better,' he said.

Anna and Jamie headed for the high street to grab a pizza before the show started at the cinema.

'So how do you know all that stuff about famous people with scoliosis?' he asked.

'I looked it up,' she said. 'Actually, I do the same for some of the conditions I know really get our patients down, and it kind of makes the kids feel a bit better that someone famous, someone whose name they actually recognise, has managed to deal with having that same condition. And I guess it makes them feel a little bit less alone.'

'It's a really good idea,' he said.

'I managed to observe the op for a few minutes during my lunch break,' she said, 'and it was fascinating. I don't often get to see surgeons at work.'

'Maybe we could look at some kind of formal enrichment process on the ward,' Jamie said. 'Your team can see what we do and ask us whatever you like, and we can learn from you about the kind of things our patients face post-op and see if there's anything we can tweak to make their recovery easier for them.'

'Good idea,' Anna agreed. 'Let's talk to Robert about it.'

When they'd eaten, they walked together up the hill to the Alexandra Palace; the massive building with its iconic transmission mast loomed up from the far side of the park.

'I really didn't expect to see so much of the City of London from here,' Jamie said when they were at the top of the hill next to the palace. 'It's a bit like Primrose Hill—the skyline's instantly recognisable, with the Shard and the Walkie-Talkie. It's gorgeous.'

'It's a great view. It's also brilliant for watching fireworks,' she said.

They went into the complex and took their seats in the theatre.

'This is amazing,' Jamie said, looking

around the room. 'Is it as old as it looks, or is it a clever modern interpretation of something that used to be here?'

'It's an original Victorian theatre,' she explained. 'It was closed to the public for eighty years and it's only just been restored and reopened. They do all sorts of things here— stage plays, the odd pop-up cinema, concerts. During the restoration, my parents made a donation for each of us for Christmas, so our names are all on a board in the foyer.' She smiled. 'It's so nice to feel we've been part of that.'

'Does your family live locally?' he asked.

She nodded. 'My parents still live in the house where we grew up, though we're trying to persuade them to move to something a little bit smaller and easier to manage. We all love it around here, so we all ended up moving back after we'd finished uni. I trained at the London Victoria, but I've worked at Muswell Hill Memorial Hospital ever since I qualified.'

The more Jamie heard about Anna's family, the more he liked the sound of them; and the more guilty he felt for pushing his own family away. His parents and sisters would love this place, he knew.

He looked up at the ceiling. 'That's stunning. I had no idea this was even here. Thanks for organising this.'

'My pleasure.' She looked slightly awkward. 'Um, I hope you don't mind that the film's a bit on the girly side.'

Love, Actually. He'd seen the posters for it in the foyer. 'I haven't actually seen it in full,' he admitted, 'though it's my sisters' favourite Christmas film.'

'Mine, too. I had a massive crush on Hugh Grant and years ago my best friend made me a life-sized cardboard cut-out of him,' she said with a smile. Then her smile faded. 'It got damaged when I moved in with Johnny and it couldn't be repaired. Looking back, I think the damage probably wasn't an accident. It should've made me see then that Johnny might not have been a keeper.'

Her ex had broken her cardboard cut-out—a gift from her best friend that had been a bit of fun to make Anna smile? How mean-spirited, Jamie thought. 'You weren't tempted to name your goldfish after Hugh?' he asked. 'Or even Grant the Goldfish, if you wanted to keep the alliteration.'

'Nope. George is named after my first love.'

'You named him after your ex-boyfriend?' Jamie asked, surprised.

'First love,' she corrected. 'George Michael. Mum used to play Wham! all the time when we were kids. I listen to Wham! now if I'm in a bad mood. Dancing around the kitchen and singing into my hairbrush is the quickest way to get me smiling again. And it's even better if I've got a niece or nephew with me. We all love singing and bopping around the room to-gether, hairbrushes in hand.'

He could just imagine it. Anna Maskell would throw herself into the singing whole-heartedly—just as she did with everything else. And he could just see her with her nieces and nephews, encouraging them and spend-ing time having fun with them.

She would've made a brilliant mother. What a shame she hadn't had the chance.

He was sitting very close to her and it would be, oh, so easy to reach out and take her hand. To hold her hand throughout the film. Every nerve in his body told him to do it.

But he remembered what she'd told him: she wasn't looking for a relationship. So it wouldn't be fair to put that kind of pressure on her. Even though he thought her ex had been utterly selfish, and her infertility wasn't a problem for Jamie in the way it clearly had been for her ex. In an odd way, it kind of made her safe to date, because it meant there was absolutely no way he could lose her in the way that he'd lost Hestia—but he rather thought that made him just as selfish as Anna's ex. And that wasn't who he was.

Anna was really family-orientated; although on the surface she seemed to have come to terms with her infertility, Jamie had a feeling that underneath maybe it wasn't so clear-cut and she still really wanted a family of her own. In his experience, pregnancy meant taking a huge risk. It had cost him everything—the love of his life, his baby, his peace of mind—and he wasn't sure he had the courage to take that kind of risk again. So he really wasn't the right one for Anna. Even though he wanted her, he needed to be unselfish about this.

He tried to concentrate on the film, but he found himself glancing at Anna every so often. He could see her face clearly in the light from the screen, and she was obviously enjoying the film hugely. He thought it was a bit daft, and it was probably more the sort of film she would've enjoyed more with her female friends, but he didn't really mind it.

Until they got to the scenes with the school Christmas concert.

Until the girl came on the stage and sang That Song. The one that always broke his heart. Although the young actress's performance was brilliant, the song just brought back so many memories for him that he felt as if he was drowning.

He glanced to the side; thankfully, Anna hadn't noticed. And he'd make damn sure that he was absolutely fine before the lights went up in the theatre so she didn't notice and feel guilty. He'd smile his head off, even though right at that moment he wanted to howl.

As they filed out into the foyer, Anna said, 'I think the school concert's my favourite bit in the film—well, that and when Colin Firth's character tries to speak Portuguese and is endearingly pants at it.' She grinned. 'But the Christmas lobster—that's genius. Which reminds me, I was going to ask you: would you like to come to the Christmas concert at my nieces' and nephew's school next week? The three middle ones are performing. They've done rehearsals at my parents' place and I can't wait to see them in costume. Aria's a shepherd in the Reception class nativity, Charlie's a robin in his class's special dance, and Megan's got the board for the partridge in the pear tree for her class's song, so she'll be leading the line on the front of the stage.'

'Thank you for inviting me, but I'm afraid I can't make it.'

How did he know? She hadn't given him a date. Anna really hadn't expected him to balk at a school Christmas concert. But something in his eyes warned her it wasn't because he was busy. 'What's wrong?' she asked quietly.

He shook his head again, clearly not wanting to discuss it in public.

'Let's go back to mine for a hot drink,' she said, and shepherded him through the park and back to her flat. She didn't push him to make conversation, because she could see he was struggling.

He stopped at her gate. 'Thank you for this evening,' he said politely. 'I'll see you tomorrow.'

'No, you'll come in and have a mug of tea or something with me,' she said, 'because I have a feeling that right now you could do with some company.'

'I…'

'Jamie, I'm not going to hurt you,' she said gently. 'I want to help. And sometimes it's easier to cope with something that's upset you if you share it with someone else.' Her counsellor had taught her that. 'Whatever you say won't go any further than me.'

Thankfully, that made him walk through her gate.

She ushered him into the kitchen. 'What can I get you? Tea? Coffee?'

'I don't mind. Anything,' he said.

It was so obvious that he was trying not to be difficult. And he was struggling. She'd had days like that herself. She made them both a mug of hot chocolate, then led him through to the living room.

'Let me introduce you. This is George the Gorgeous Goldfish. George, this is my friend from work, Jamie.'

'Hi, George,' Jamie said, but his voice was a flat monotone, worrying her even more; she'd hoped that the sheer incongruity of being introduced to a goldfish might at least make him smile and put a crack in the wall he seemed to be building round himself.

Clearly not. So how was she going to break through to him?

She thought about it. He'd chatted to her before the film, and she was fairly sure he'd enjoyed the film itself—but he'd gone really quiet when she'd asked him to the concert. That had to be the problem. She didn't know how to make this better; and she was scared that whatever she said might make things worse. On the other hand, she couldn't just leave him to the thoughts that were clearly ripping him to shreds.

She gestured to him to sit on the sofa, and sat down next to him. 'Jamie, I'm really sorry if I'm treading on a sore spot, because that's not my intention,' she said, 'but the school Christmas concert seems to be the thing that's really upset you and I don't understand why. I don't want to make things worse, so please can you help me understand what it is?'

She'd been honest with him, Jamie thought. So now it was time for him to be honest with her.

'It wasn't the concert, exactly. It was the film,' he said. 'That song. "All I Want for

Christmas is You". It was Hestia's—my wife's—favourite song, and she'd sing it all round the house in December.' He took a deep breath. 'She died. So did our baby. Just over three years ago.' The anniversary had been the week before he'd started at the Muswell Hill Memorial Hospital. 'If they'd still been alive, this year would've been the first year we'd have gone to nursery school for a Christmas concert.'

It was the first time he'd actually said it out loud for a long, long time. Usually it was like a bruise in his soul, there all the time, aching and never reaching the surface.

And now he'd actually said it out loud, he didn't know what to do. What to say next.

Every instinct told him to run.

And he couldn't look at Anna. He couldn't bear to see the pity on her face.

As if she'd guessed what he was thinking—or, more likely, it was written all over his expression—she took his hand and squeezed it briefly, before letting it go. 'The last thing you need right now is pity, and I'm not pitying you at all, but I do sympathise. It's hard enough to lose people you love, but Christmas has to be the worst time of all for it to happen.'

Yeah. She could say that again. Everyone else seemed to be celebrating, talking about love and peace and happiness, and all that had been around him that year had been death and sadness. And he got sucked into it every year. Christmas was supposed to be a time of joy, but for him it was a time of shadows and he didn't know how to break the cycle.

'I understand now why you don't like Christmas,' she said quietly, 'and I'm so sorry I've been insensitive. I'm your colleague and I hope I'm becoming your friend. If you want to talk, I'm here—and, just in case you're worrying, I have absolutely no intention of betraying your confidence and making you the hot topic on the hospital grapevine.'

He knew that. She wasn't the type to spread gossip.

'In my experience,' she said, 'talking about difficult things kind of cuts them down to size and stops them being overwhelming. When I found out about my infertility, I was devastated. It felt as if my life didn't have any point, if I couldn't have children. I didn't feel as if I was a real woman, because I couldn't do what every other woman in the world seemed to be able to do. But you know Jenna Conti on our ward? Her twin sister Lucy had a serious accident a few years ago that meant she couldn't have children, and Jenna was her surrogate mum and had a baby for her. Jenna introduced me to Lucy, so I had someone to talk to who actually understood what it was like to have your choices taken away. Lucy and Jenna both really helped me.'

Someone who understood. Someone who'd been in her shoes.

Jamie didn't know anyone who'd been in his shoes. Nobody who'd been a widower or a widow in their early thirties; nobody who'd lost their partner and their baby to eclampsia.

'And you've lost someone?' He knew it was bitter and he hated himself for it, but he couldn't call the words back now.

'My grandparents,' she said, 'and I've been lucky because they had a long and happy life and, even though I'm sad they're no longer around, it felt as if it was in the natural order of things. But my best friend lost her mum to breast cancer, so I understand how people feel when they lose someone too soon. It's not the things you did or said, it's the things you didn't have time to do or say.'

Her words resonated with him. He hadn't

even had the chance to say goodbye to Hestia. And it wasn't the same, sitting in a hospital morgue with someone you knew for definite couldn't hear you saying goodbye, someone who couldn't squeeze your hand one last time. It wasn't at all like being with someone right at the end, holding them and telling them you loved them, making sure they weren't alone as they slid into unconsciousness and then death.

He'd let Hestia down because he hadn't been there when she'd died.

He looked at Anna then, and there wasn't a trace of pity on her face. Fellow-feeling, sympathy and kindness, yes, but not pity. He opened his mouth, and suddenly the words blurted out. 'Hestia had eclampsia.'

She looked sad, but said nothing. Though she did take his hand again. She wasn't holding his hand like a lover; she was holding his hand like someone who cared what he said, who was going to give him the space to think about what he said, and who wasn't going anywhere until he'd talked.

So he talked.

'She was seven months pregnant and she'd just gone on maternity leave. Our baby was due the week before Christmas. Hestia was on her way to the corner shop to get a pint of milk. She collapsed in the middle of the street and had a seizure. And I often think, maybe if I'd checked the cupboards before I went to work and got some milk so she hadn't had to go out…' He shook his head.

'Which I know is ridiculous, because obviously it would've happened anyway. Just she would've been at home instead of outside. And nobody would've called an ambulance, because nobody would've known she'd collapsed or was having a seizure, so in a way that would've been even worse. At least she wasn't alone at the very end—there were people nearby who helped her.' He raked a hand through his hair.

'The ambulance came quickly, but she'd had a cerebral haemorrhage and she died in the ambulance on the way to the emergency department. Our daughter Giselle died, too. It was too late to do a C-section to save the baby.'

'Your worst nightmare,' she said softly.

One he'd never woken up from.

'I'm sorry that something so terrible happened to your wife and baby,' she said.

'And I wasn't there with them at the end.

That's the worst bit,' Jamie said. 'I know Hestia loved me, and I loved her, but I can't help feeling I let her down.'

'Were you at work when it happened?'

He nodded. 'I was in the operating theatre. She was even brought into the hospital where I worked—but it was another three hours until I got the message from the Emergency Department.'

'That's not your fault,' she said. 'And even if you'd got the message in Theatre, you could hardly have dropped everything and left your patient on the table.'

'Leaving my junior to carry on with an operation that was outside his experience and putting unfair pressure on the whole team, and letting the patient down as well. In my head, I know that,' he said. 'But another part of me still feels I failed my wife. I'm a *doctor*, for pity's sake. I should've noticed that something was wrong before I left for work that morning.'

'You're an orthopaedic surgeon, not an obstetrician,' she reminded him. 'OK, yes, as a doctor you would either know the symptoms of the really scary pregnancy complications or you would've looked them up—but you can't know everything about everyone else's specialties. Nobody can.'

Technically, that was true. He knew that. Emotionally, he still felt he'd let Hestia down.

'Did she have any symptoms of pre-eclampsia, or was she at high risk?' Anna asked.

Jamie shook his head. 'She wasn't diabetic, she didn't have kidney problems or high blood pressure or anything else that would make her more susceptible to pre-eclampsia, and there wasn't a family history of pre-eclampsia or any difficulties at all during pregnancy. Her blood pressure was fine; there was a tiny bit of protein in her urine at her last appointment, but the midwife wasn't overly concerned and was going to do a check at her next appointment.' The appointment two days after her death. 'Hestia hadn't mentioned any headaches either.'

'Then you're really not being very fair to yourself,' Anna said. 'You can't possibly diagnose a condition if there aren't any symptoms. And remember eclampsia's called that for a reason: it's a lightning strike.'

From the Greek. He remembered.

'It's something that you simply can't predict.'

'One in four thousand pregnancies.' He knew every horrible statistic. Death in pregnancy or childbirth was so much less common nowadays; but shockingly one in fifty women with eclampsia died, and of the babies one in fourteen died.

Hestia and Giselle had both been on the wrong side of the statistics.

'I'm sorry,' she said. 'And it must be hard for you, working in paediatrics and seeing children who are the same age as your daughter would've been now.'

'Weirdly, it's easier at work,' he said. 'Because the children we see are ill and we're making them better. I can cope with that. It's...' He blew out a breath. 'It's seeing children outside. That's hard. All the might-have-beens.'

'Then I won't push you to come to my nieces' and nephew's Christmas concert,' she said. 'That'll be too much for you.'

'Isn't it hard for you, too?' he asked. 'Seeing people with babies and toddlers? All the might-have-beens?'

'It was, at one point,' she said. 'But I'm lucky that my family and friends are really generous. I'm godmother to several of my friends' children. They all include me in things they do with the kids, so I get to do most of what I would've done with my own children, if I'd been that lucky. I go to swimming class or to toddler music class, I get invites to all the nursery and school shows, I get to do bed-time stories and all the fun bits of parenting like afternoons at the park, days at the beach or trips to the sea life centres.' She gave him a wry smile. 'Not just the fun bits, though. I've had my share of changing poomageddon nappies, too.'

'Poomageddon?' he asked, mystified.

'That was my nephew Noah, when he had gastric flu last year and Jojo and Becky went down with it as well. I looked after the three of them, dispensing lots of drinks, paracetamol and cool flannels. The nappies were, you might say, a bit on the challenging side. But we managed.'

And Jamie had had longer to come to terms with his wife and baby's death than Anna had had to come to terms with her infertility and a husband who'd had an affair and a baby with someone else, letting her down.

Then he realised he'd spoken aloud. 'I'm s—'

'Shh.' She pressed her forefinger lightly

against his lips. 'Don't apologise. There isn't a time limit on grief, and we're not in a competition over who's had the toughest deal. Things are as they are. And maybe I've had more support than you have. I'm really lucky with my family.'

'Mine are good, too,' he said. And that was something else he felt guilty about. 'Except I've pushed them away. I use work as an excuse not to see them very often, and I always make sure I'm on duty on Christmas Day so I don't have to face them—they're all so kind and so careful not to say anything that might upset me, and I hate the fact they feel they have to tread on eggshells around me. They wrap me in so much cotton wool that it suffocates me. I know it looks as if I'm being selfish, abandoning them and wallowing in misery—but, the way I see it, if I'm not there, then they can have fun without worrying about accidentally upsetting me.'

'Then maybe,' she said, 'we should carry on with our Christmas deal. Take the sting out of it for you so you can cope with it again and make things up with your family so you can enjoy each other's company.'

'That's what I want to do,' he said. 'Just…' It was so hard. As if he'd put an unscaleable wall around himself and he didn't know how to get out again.

'And we'll make sure we avoid that song. Though,' she pointed out, 'it's the one song that probably gets the most airplay at this time of year, so it's really not going to be easy to avoid it.'

'I know.'

'It's not the same as my situation with Johnny,' she said. 'But, if he'd been the man I thought he was when I married him, and he was the one who'd been left behind, I would've wanted him to find happiness again. To meet someone who could give him the love I didn't have time to give. And I'm guessing that Hestia would've hated the idea of you cutting yourself off from everyone and being lonely for the rest of your life.'

'She would,' he admitted. 'And I think that's why I agreed to your Christmas bargain. Because I really do want to move on from the past and make things right again with my family—and hers—but I just don't know where to start.'

'With my family,' she said, 'a text would do. All I'd have to say is "I'm having a bit of trouble dealing with this, but please bear with me because I love you and I'm trying to find my way back somehow", and they'd understand. They'd give me space for a while and then try to meet me halfway. Though I also know not every family's like mine.'

'I think mine are. But it's been so long,' he said. 'It's too late.'

'It's never too late. Call them. Text them or write to them if you don't think you'll be able to say the words,' she said. 'Because my guess is they've tried to give you space and now they don't know how to reach you either, and they're as scared of that huge gulf as you are. They're worried that if they reach out they'll accidentally push you further away. So don't let that gap get any bigger. You don't have to reach the whole way across, just some of the way. And, from what you've just told me, I'm pretty sure they'll reach right back to meet you.'

He had no idea how Anna had got so wise, but he was grateful.

'You could,' she said, 'text them now.'

He glanced at his watch. 'It's a bit late. I wouldn't want them to think it was an emergency and start worrying.'

'Do it tomorrow, then. Before you go to work. Then you'll have a valid reason not to look at your phone all day, because you're operating. It gives you all a bit of space.'

'Thank you,' he said. 'For listening. For talking sense into me. For putting up with me being such a mess.'

'That's what friends are for,' she said. 'And I think you'd do the same for me if our positions were reversed.'

He thought about it. 'Yes. I would. I don't think I'm as good with people as you are... But I'd try.'

'Well, then.' She smiled at him. 'Go home.'

'And plan what I'm going to say, right?'

'Right. Just keep it simple and honest,' she said, and released his hand.

Which was probably just as well, because he was very tempted to wrap his arms round her. To hold her. And it wasn't just gratitude. It was other feelings prompting him, things he wasn't used to feeling and which scared him and thrilled him in equal measure.

And then there was the guilt. How could he even be noticing another woman like this, when he'd just spilled out his heart about losing Hestia? Even though he knew Hestia wouldn't have wanted him to spend the rest of his life grieving for her and he needed to move on, it still felt like a betrayal of sorts.

He needed to get his head together. Be cool, logical and unflappable, like the surgeon he was at work. 'OK. I'll see you tomorrow.'

'You bet.'

He walked back to his flat, and her words echoed in his head all the way.

'If he'd been the man I thought he was when I married him, and he was the one who'd been left behind, I would've wanted him to find happiness again. To meet someone who could give him the love I didn't have time to give.'

Jamie knew that was what Hestia would've wanted for him, too. She would've been furious that he'd wallowed in despair for three years.

Find happiness.

Meet someone.

All the breath suddenly left his lungs when he realised that he *had* met someone. Someone who was changing the way he was seeing the world and was teaching him to find happiness. Someone who'd been through the mill herself. Anna Maskell was bringing light back into his life; and maybe, just maybe, he could be the one who did the same for her.

He thought about that all the rest of the way home.

And then it was easy to write those texts to his family. Keeping the words simple and heartfelt and honest.

Hi. I'm sorry I've shut you out for the last three years. I've been finding it hard coming to terms with Hestia and Giselle dying. But I want you to know I love you and I'm trying to find my way back to some kind of normal. Please don't give up on me.

He waited until the morning to send them, not wanting to worry anyone with a late-night message.

What he hadn't expected was how quickly the replies came, his phone pinging almost immediately after he'd sent them. His mother, his sisters, his mother-in-law, Hestia's sister. And they were all variations on a theme.

I love you too and I'm here whenever you're ready to talk.

Tears filled his eyes. Anna had been right. His family were all ready to reach out over that gulf, to meet him halfway. But, without her pushing him, he would never have been able to make that first step and reach out to them.

Anna Maskell, he decided, was getting the biggest bouquet of flowers ever.

He didn't manage to see her during the day, because she was busy with clinic and ward rounds and he was in Theatre, so instead he texted her during a break.

You busy tonight?

The reply came back.

Sorry. Going to Zumba with my sister-in-law and then a family dinner.

So he couldn't call round to her place tonight with the flowers, then.

His phone pinged again with another message from Anna.

Am free tomorrow, if you want to do something.

This was his chance to move on. Instead of leaving all the Christmas stuff to her, he could make an effort. Suggest something. Meet her halfway.

Maybe we can go and see some Christmas lights?

The Regent Street angels?

That's fine. I'll meet you at your flat at seven. Maybe we can grab dinner, before or after.

Love to.

It wasn't a date, he reminded himself. It was just part of their Christmas bargain. Except maybe now he could start to move forward and do things for her, too. Help her move past the hurt Johnny had inflicted and see just what an amazing woman she was.

Any man would be lucky to have Anna Maskell as his partner.

Could he be that man?

Although part of him was terrified at the idea of opening himself up to another relationship and risking the possibility of loss, another part of him wanted to be that man. Because the alternative was Anna meeting someone else and settling down with him. Jamie wanted Anna to be happy, but the thought of it being with someone who wasn't him made him feel miserable.

He needed to do the right thing by her. Help her see how wonderful she was, give her the courage to move past Johnny's betrayal and give her heart to someone who deserved her. A man who could give her the family she wanted, deep down.

And he wanted to be the man who deserved her. Did he have the courage to take that risk? Given her infertility, any pregnancy would be extremely high risk—if the treatment even worked in the first place. IVF had no guarantees. Even suggesting it was like offering false hope, something he might not be able to deliver. But there were other options. Surrogacy. Fostering. Adoption,

Could he move on and risk loving again?

Could he make Anna happy?

Or should he put her first and just back off?

CHAPTER SEVEN

ON WEDNESDAY MORNING Anna saw Lily during her ward rounds, then called back in later to see her with a sudoku magazine.

Lily beamed. 'That's really nerdy—and really kind. Thank you. I love these sorts of puzzles.'

'Pleasure.' Anna smiled back at her. 'Well, hey, I was wondering what a maths wizard might like to do to pass the time between visitors—and hopefully you'll make some friends on the ward, too, so you can chat to people here.'

'Jamie came to see me earlier,' Lily said. 'Mum helped me get out of bed and I took two whole steps in front of him, and he was really pleased.'

'I bet he was. Keep up the good work. The physio's coming back to see you this afternoon,' Anna said with a smile.

Jamie.

She still couldn't quite believe that he'd actually suggested doing a Christmas thing rather than leaving all the plans to her. Was this a sign that he was starting to heal and getting ready to move on? Was Christmas finally losing its sting for him?

She really hoped that he'd contacted his family; and she hoped even more that they'd reacted the same way her family would have reacted, reaching back out to him.

Though she was going to have to be careful. Jamie had lost his wife and child; so it was a fair bet that, when he was ready to move on again, he'd want someone who could give him a family without complications. Which meant moving on with someone other than her. She couldn't afford to think of Jamie Thurston as anything other than a friend and a colleague— no matter how tempting his gorgeous blue eyes and shy smile were.

Her life was full and it was good. Plenty of people struggled on with far more problems than she had. Wanting more was simply greedy, and she'd count her blessings.

At five to seven that evening, Jamie stood outside Anna's front door, holding an enormous bouquet of flowers. He'd ordered them from a local florist the previous day, asking for something pretty and Christmassy. The florist had made an arrangement with deep red roses, cream-coloured freesias, and then eryngium that had been sprayed silver, teamed with the silvery green foliage of eucalyptus and the deeper green leaves of laurel.

He rang the bell; a few moments later, she opened the door, smiling a welcome at him. 'Hey. Perfect timing. I'm just about to put my boots on and find wherever I put my gloves.'

'These are for you,' he said, and handed her the bouquet. 'I hope you like them.'

'For me? Thank you. They're absolutely gorgeous. I love them.' Her eyes widened. 'But it's not my birthday or anything.'

'It's because you've really helped me and I wanted to say thank you.'

'Oh.' Her cheeks flushed, making her look incredibly pretty. He really wanted to kiss her, right there and then, but he held himself back.

'So does that mean we've done enough festive things now to make this time of year easier for you, and you're going to be my Father Christmas on the ward?' she asked.

'I'm still thinking about it. I'm not *quite* ready to say yes,' he said.

Though what he wasn't admitting, even to himself, was that he didn't want his Christmassy trips with Anna to end. He was starting to look forward to them, and it wasn't just that she was taking the sting out of Christmas for him. It was because he enjoyed her company. Being with her made the world feel like a much warmer, sweeter place. He liked who he was when he was with her. But was he being selfish? Should he step aside and let her find someone who really could bring her happiness, someone without all the emotional baggage and complications that came with him? Or, with her help, could he become the man who'd bring her the joy she deserved?

'OK. I need to put these in water before we go out. Come in while I grab a vase.'

In her kitchen, Jamie noticed all the children's paintings held onto the door of her fridge with magnets. He hadn't noticed them on Monday night, when he'd still been numb and despairing; but now he could see how much she was loved by her nieces and nephews, and how much she clearly loved them.

'These flowers really are spectacular,' she

said, filling a vase and putting the bouquet into water. 'I still don't think I've done anything special to deserve them, but I really appreciate them.'

'Actually, you've done way more than you think,' he said. 'I texted my mum, my sisters and Hestia's mum and sister yesterday morning just before I left for work. Like you suggested, I kept it simple and honest. I apologised for pushing them away and said I was finding it hard to deal with what happened, but I wanted to let them know that I loved them.'

'Good,' she said. Then she met his gaze head-on. 'Did they reply?'

'All of them. Before I'd even got halfway to the hospital.' He could still hardly believe it, and shook his head in wonderment. 'All of them said they loved me, too, and would be there whenever I wanted to see them or talk. They understood and they'd wait until I was ready.'

'I'm glad,' she said.

So was he.

They headed out to see the Christmas lights in Regent Street: angels with enormous wings and draping skirts made from twinkly lights. Jamie couldn't help thinking of Hestia, and the times he'd seen her on stage wearing an ankle-length gauzy skirt; how often he'd thought she'd danced like an angel. Looking up at the lights, he almost felt as if she approved of what he was doing. That he was looking to rejoin the world and find happiness again.

'They're glorious. Apparently it's a nod to the very first Christmas lights that were put up here in the nineteen-fifties,' she said, 'because they were angels, too.'

As they walked down towards Bond Street, their hands brushed against each other. Once, twice; the third time, Jamie couldn't help catching Anna's fingers loosely in his. She didn't pull away; and gradually, as they walked, he let his fingers mesh more closely with hers until they were really holding hands.

This was how Anna remembered feeling as a teen, with her skin tingling with nerves and excitement as she held her boyfriend's hand for the very first time.

Except she was thirty-four, not fourteen. And Jamie Thurston wasn't a skinny boy with terrible skin and greasy hair. They'd both had their hearts broken and were at different stages of putting the pieces back together.

If she had any sense, she'd make some excuse to drop his hand—fake-sneezing into a tissue or something like that—and she'd chatter brightly to him and keep him at a distance. Firmly in the friend zone. This wasn't a date.

But, for the life of her, right at that moment she couldn't help holding his hand just as tightly as he was holding hers.

They strolled down to Bond Street to see the peacock-inspired lights, the beautiful fan-shaped display spanning the whole street at one end, and then individual peacock feathers peeking out from behind them in silver and gold, the 'eye' of the feather gradually changing colour.

Speaking would break the spell, she thought, so she said nothing until they turned into a side street and found a pop-up Christmas street food market.

'Shall we?' Jamie asked—though he didn't let go of her hand.

Food. He meant food. He wasn't talking about kissing her under non-existent mistletoe, Anna reminded herself, even though her lips were tingling slightly in anticipation.

'Dinner sounds good,' she said, hearing the huskiness in her own voice and wincing slightly.

He was still holding her hand as they chose dinner—Christmas spiced turkey empanadas with cranberry chilli salsa, which tasted even better than they sounded, and then rich squares of Christmas pudding brownie, sprayed gold and with a swirl of cinnamon cream and a glacé cherry on top.

He held her hand again all the way back to the Tube station, all the way back on the train, and all the way from the station to her front door.

'Thank you for a lovely evening,' he said.

'I enjoyed it, too.' She paused. 'Do you want to come in for coffee?'

Her hair was loose, and he tucked a strand behind her ear. 'Yes. And no.'

She frowned. 'Is that some weird kind of surgical puzzle?'

'It's me saying I want to spend time with you, but it's complicated and it's probably fairer to both of us if I don't.'

She looked down at their joined hands. 'I see.' Which was totally untrue. She was more confused than ever. Was this a thing, or wasn't it? Were they friends, or finding their way towards something else?

He kissed her cheek. 'This scares the hell out of me. You're the first person who's made me feel anything at all since Hestia died.

Which is a good thing—but it's also something I need to get my head around.'

'I haven't dated anyone since Johnny,' she admitted. And in some ways Jamie was the worst man she could date. Being with him was a huge risk. He'd already lost so much. Would she be enough for him? What if he decided further down the line that he wanted a child of his own? That would put her right back in the same place she'd been with Johnny, unable to give her man the one thing he really wanted: a baby. And, although she didn't think Jamie would deliberately hurt her, she'd once believed that about Johnny. Could she really trust her judgement?

Or maybe she was overthinking this. 'Though tonight wasn't a date.'

'Agreed. It was part of our Christmas bargain. But if you drew a Venn diagram I think there would be quite a crossover.' This time, Jamie kissed the corner of her mouth.

She rested her palm against his cheek. 'So we're going to take this slowly. See where it goes. Just between you and me. No pushing, no rushing, no pressure.' Less risk, though she wasn't quite brave enough to admit that.

'That works for me.' He took a deep breath. 'You're going indoors now and I'm going back to my own place. As you said, no rushing. Just…' He wrapped his free arm around her and held her close. 'See you tomorrow.'

She wrapped her free arm around him, still holding his hand and enjoying the closeness. 'See you tomorrow.'

And funny how the world seemed different, the colours brighter.

On Friday morning, Anna and Jamie were in clinic with Michael Jeffries, a teenager who'd been caught up in a bad tackle during a football game and had torn his anterior cruciate ligament.

'I saw the other doctor,' he said, 'and she said I'd torn my ACL but there was a lot of swelling, so I had to wait for that to go down and a full range of movement to return before she could even think of operating.' He grimaced. 'I couldn't even turn on the spot. She said I could do swimming and have physio for the last month to keep my quads and my hams strong, but I wasn't allowed to do anything where I'd turn, jump or twist.'

'Which must've made you a bit stir-crazy,' Anna said sympathetically.

'Yeah. I hated it. I couldn't wait for today. Football's my life,' Michael said. 'Please tell me you're going to be able to fix my knee. I've got a place at the football academy. If I can't play, they'll give it to someone else and I'll be out. I'll have lost...' He shook his head, clearly close to tears.

Anna glanced at Jamie, willing him to give the boy some hope.

'The good news is I can fix your knee,' Jamie said, 'but the bad news is that you're not going to recover overnight. It'll take at least six months, and realistically it could be as much as a year before you can return to full training.'

'A whole *year*?' Michael looked horrified.

'A year,' Jamie said. 'And let's be very clear about this—if you go back to training before you're ready, you could do more damage to your knee, to the point where I wouldn't be able to fix it next time.'

Michael stared at them, his eyes wide. 'If I can't play football, my life might as well be over. I've never wanted to do anything else. I...' He blew out a breath. 'I have to play. I *have* to.'

'You'll be able to play again,' Jamie said, 'provided you give yourself proper recovery time.'

'Do you want your dad to come in?' Anna asked gently.

Michael shook his head. 'He'll be so disappointed in me.'

'It's not your fault you got hurt in a tackle,' Jamie reminded him. He brought the scan image up onto the screen of his computer and tilted the screen so Michael could see it. 'You can see the damage for yourself. The ligament's torn very badly.'

'So what are you going to do? Sew it back together?' Michael asked.

Jamie shook his head. 'I'll need to graft new tissue. What I'll do is remove the torn ligament and replace it with a bit of your patellar tendon—that's the tendon that attaches the bottom of your kneecap to the top of your shinbone.'

'And that will definitely fix it?'

'Provided you don't have damage to the cartilage that I can't see on the scan—I'll only be able to see that when I look inside your knee,' Jamie said.

Michael took a deep breath. 'All right. Will I have to stay in hospital?'

'Overnight, yes,' Jamie said. 'I'm going to do keyhole surgery. It'll take about an hour and a half, maybe a bit more, depending on how much damage I need to fix. And it's up to you whether you'd rather have a general anaesthetic so you're asleep throughout the whole thing, or if you want a spinal block so you'll be conscious during the actual operation and you'll know what's going on around you but you won't feel any pain.'

Michael looked nervous. 'I... Can I choose on the day?'

'The day before might be better,' Jamie said. 'And I think your dad needs to come in now, so I can talk you both through exactly what I'm going to do.'

'He's going to be so disappointed in me,' Michael said again.

'More like he's going to be worrying himself sick out there, wanting to know if you'll be all right,' Anna said gently.

Michael shook his head. 'If I wasn't any good at football, he wouldn't bother with me. He doesn't bother with my sister. All he cares about is—' He stopped abruptly.

Football? Anna wondered. But it wasn't her place to judge. 'OK,' she said, then went to the door and called Michael's father in.

'So when can he play again?' Mr Jeffries asked.

Nothing about whether Michael would be out of pain or what he could do to help his son, Anna noticed. This was a man whose priorities were very different from what her own would've been.

'He can play again when he's recovered properly,' Jamie said crisply, 'and that depends on how much damage there is to the cartilage, which I'll only be able to see when I operate. The important thing is that he's going to be out of pain.'

Mr Jeffries's eyes narrowed. 'Yes.'

Had Michael not let slip that comment about his sister, Anna would've thought that maybe his father was worried about how Michael would cope with having to wait until he could play again, because football was the boy's big passion. But now she wondered how much Michael really loved football for its own sake, and how much of it was a way of trying to connect with his father.

'We asked you to come in,' she said, 'so Mr Thurston could explain the operation to you both. If you have any questions about the best way to support your son's recovery, we'll be very happy to help.'

Mr Jeffries looked at her as if she was merely a decoration.

This wasn't about her, but she didn't appreciate his attitude. If he treated any of her team like that, she'd be having a stern word with him about the hospital's zero tolerance policy.

'I'm going to use a thin, flexible tube called an arthroscope,' Jamie explained. 'It has fibre optic cables inside so it acts as both a camera and a light, to show me your knee joint. I'll examine the inside of your knee and repair any damage to the cartilage. It'll confirm that your ACL is torn, Michael, so then I'll remove the graft tissue and cut it to the right size.'

'Where does the graft tissue come from?' Mr Jeffries asked.

'From the tendon that attaches his shinbone to his kneecap,' Jamie said.

'Why can't he just have physiotherapy? Surgery means he's going to be out of the team for months.' Mr Jeffries started at Jamie. 'He might lose his place at the football academy.'

'Physiotherapy on its own isn't enough. Michael's anterior cruciate ligament is badly torn, and that means he needs surgery to stabilise his knee,' Jamie explained patiently. 'Without it he'll be in considerable pain—and playing football will be completely out of the question.'

Mr Jeffries didn't look happy, but said nothing.

'Once I've removed your torn ligament, Michael, I'll make a tunnel in your bone to pass the new tissue through, and then I'll screw the graft tissue in place—it'll act as a scaffold for the new ligament to grow across, and will stay in your knee permanently. Once I'm happy it's strong enough to hold your knee together, it's stable and you've got the full range of movement in your knee, then I'll sew you up, put on a dressing and let you recover. And then, if you've chosen to have a general anaesthetic rather than a spinal block, we'll wake you up.'

'I think,' Michael said, 'I'd rather be asleep during the operation.'

'That's fine. And it's fine to change your mind if you think about it and then decide you'd rather be awake,' Jamie said. 'I'll use dissolvable stitches, so they'll disappear after about three weeks and you won't have to come back to have them removed.' He flicked a glance at Mr Jeffries, who remained utterly silent.

'Your knee will be a bit swollen and bruised for the first week and it will hurt,' Jamie continued, 'but we'll give you painkillers to help with that, and give you a special bandage that has iced water inside so it will help with the swelling. We'll give you some exercises to start off your recovery, and it's a good idea to use crutches for the first couple of weeks. Then you'll need to keep up with your physio for the next six months.'

'And then he can start playing?' Mr Jeffries demanded.

'That,' Jamie said, 'depends on how he heals. Everyone's different. I'd be guided by what the physio says.'

Mr Jeffries rolled his eyes. 'A couple of sports massages will sort it out.'

'I think you'll find,' Anna said, 'that any coach and any therapist will take the same view as the surgeon. Michael's health comes first. If he goes back too early, he'll set his progress back and risk never being able to play again.'

Mr Jeffries gave her a look of contempt. 'And you know much about sport, do you?'

'I know a little bit about medicine,' Anna said lightly. She wasn't giving this rude, arrogant man the satisfaction of arguing with him.

'Just to reassure you, Mr Jeffries,' Jamie said, 'Dr Maskell is a highly experienced senior doctor. She's one step down from being a consultant.'

'But if you'd rather have a second opinion on Michael's treatment from the head of the department,' Anna said, 'I'm very happy to go and find him for you.' Robert would be all charm—but he'd also put this man totally in his place and make it clear that their patient's needs came way, way before anything else. And Anna really regretted her impulse to call Mr Jeffries in to support Michael. She understood now why Michael hadn't wanted his father there. The man wasn't in the least bit supportive.

'That won't be necessary,' Mr Jeffries snapped.

'Good,' Jamie said coolly. 'Michael, I can get you on my list for Wednesday.'

'Thank you.'

Once they'd gone, Anna turned to Jamie. 'Thanks for sticking up for me.'

'It was the least I could do. What an idiot.' He rolled his eyes. 'If he gives anyone on the ward any trouble, let me know.'

'Thanks. Though I think we'd all just ignore him and concentrate on Michael.'

'Good idea,' he said. 'I'll just finish my notes, then we'll see the next patient on our list.'

* * *

The rest of the day flew by. Anna was late getting home but had just enough time to put on a red velvet skater dress, high heels and make-up before heading to the pub where the department's Christmas meal was being held. She had a quiet word with the manager about the music, checked that everything else was ready for them, and then they were good to go.

Once everyone was sitting down—Jamie was next to her—and had pulled their cracker, put on their paper hat and read out the terrible jokes, the meal was served. And once everyone had eaten and was enjoying coffee and petits fours, Robert excused himself for a moment and returned wearing the Father Christmas outfit and holding a large sack marked 'Swag'. 'Ho-ho-ho,' he boomed. 'This is the moment you've all been waiting for. Have you all been good, boys and girls?'

Jamie was surprised at how much he was enjoying the evening. The food was as good as Anna had promised, and he was relieved to discover it was just a meal with no dancing. There was Christmas music playing in the background, but the chatter blocked it out, and he had a feeling that Anna might just have had a word with whoever was in charge of the music because he'd been on tenterhooks, waiting for That Song, and it didn't arrive.

He'd made the effort to chat to the rest of the people he was sitting with, and it really felt as if he fitted in. Somehow, in only three short weeks, he'd managed to become as much a part of the team as he had at the hospital in south London where he'd trained and worked until three years ago. Though he had a feeling that the reason he felt so much part of it was because Anna was there.

Robert took the parcels from the sack and dished them out in turn, waiting for the recipient to open it before moving on to the next one. Jamie had drawn Keely's name; because he didn't know her well, he'd played it safe with a set of shower gel and body butter, which had been beautifully wrapped by the shop where he'd bought it. He'd been given what he recognised as a safe gift, too: a box of mixed milk, dark and white chocolates, which he intended to share.

Other people were given more personal gifts. Whoever had drawn Anna's name had bought her a clipboard and customised it with

'Ward Social Organiser Supremo' in sparkly letters on one side, and a picture of George Michael and a goldfish on the other, which had her in fits of laughter; though it also came with a jar of very posh chocolate flakes to stir into hot milk, which he knew she'd love. Jamie thoroughly enjoyed watching everyone's reactions to their gifts, and then the hubbub of chatter afterwards.

At the end of the evening, he walked Anna home. 'Thank you for nagging me into doing this tonight,' he said. 'You're right. It was a lot of fun.' And he really hadn't expected to have such a good time.

'I'm glad you enjoyed it,' she said with a smile.

'And also I wanted to tell you I'm meeting up with my family tomorrow,' he told her.

She blinked. 'So you've talked to them since you texted them, the other day?'

He nodded. 'Shelley—my oldest sister— called me and invited me to dinner tomorrow night. It's nothing fancy, just spaghetti and garlic bread and ice cream, and my niece Layla's going to make choc-chip cookies. And on Sunday I'm going to see Hestia's family for lunch.'

'That's fabulous,' she said, looking pleased.

He almost—*almost*—asked her to go with him.

But that wouldn't be fair. He needed to fix things with his family and Hestia's first. Plus he and Anna had agreed to take things slowly. He couldn't rush her into making their Christmas deal more than just friendship.

Baby steps, he reminded himself.

Though he could still kiss her goodnight on her doorstep. And funny how right it felt to have her in his arms, her mouth soft and sweet against his. He almost wished there had been dancing at the ward's Christmas meal so he could hold her close and sway with her.

'Goodnight,' he said softly. 'I'll see you later.'

'Have a good time with your family,' she said.

'Thank you. What about you—what are you up to at the weekend?' he asked.

'Sunday lunch at my parents' place,' she said, 'and no doubt a dress rehearsal for next week's Christmas concert.' Her face was full of glee. 'I can't wait. Though I'll be working for it tomorrow, with a whole week's worth of laundry and ironing to do...'

* * *

Seeing his sister wasn't as awkward as Jamie had expected. There were no recriminations, no over-the-top reunion to make him feel like the prodigal brother: just a hug and dinner. He caught up with his brother-in-law Alex, and had long conversations with Dylan and Layla, who shyly talked to him about their love of space and baking respectively.

'I'm so sorry,' Jamie said to Shelley in the kitchen when he was helping her clear away after dinner. 'I've missed out on so much of their growing up. Dylan and Layla have changed massively over last three years. I really haven't been fair to you.'

'Don't beat yourself up about the past, just go forward,' Shelley said gently. 'The main thing is that you're getting to a better place now.'

'I am.' He told her all about his job at Muswell Hill Memorial Hospital.

'It sounds as if you've really settled in.'

He nodded. 'I could be tempted to stay for the whole of Nalini's maternity leave, not just the three months we agreed to.'

'Do it, if you're happy,' Shelley said.

At the end of the evening, they agreed to

do it again the following weekend—but this time with their parents and their middle sister there as well.

Back at his flat, Jamie looked at the photograph of Hestia on his screen-saver. It was his favourite photograph of her, a shot taken by a magazine of her performing as the Sugar Plum Fairy at Covent Garden, mid-pirouette with her arms gracefully above her head.

'I'm starting to move on, Hes,' he said softly. 'It doesn't mean I'm cutting you out of my life or pretending you never existed, but I know how cross you'd be with me for locking myself out of the world.' He paused. 'You'd like Anna. She's bright and sparkly, like the star on the top of the Christmas tree. I think she and I might be good for each other.'

Seeing Hestia's family on the Sunday, too, went better than he'd expected. It felt as if finally the misery of the last three years was starting to lose its sting and there was a light at the end of the tunnel.

Anna Maskell had made a huge difference to his life.

He hoped that he might be able to make the same kind of difference to hers.

CHAPTER EIGHT

JAMIE AND ANNA were on different shifts on Monday, so he didn't get to see her. But on Tuesday morning they were in clinic together, and their first patient was a week-old baby with talipes, a congenital condition where both feet pointed downwards and inwards with the soles of the feet facing each other.

'We've never had anything like this in either of our families,' Kirsty Peters, the mum, said. She bit her lip. 'The obstetrician said it wasn't anything I did wrong when I was pregnant, but I can't help thinking I must've done, and I hate it that Willow's in pain.'

'She's not in pain,' Anna reassured her, 'and you definitely didn't do anything wrong—in most cases we don't know what causes it.'

'The obstetrician said Willow would have to have an operation,' Kirsty said.

'It's not quite as scary as it sounds,' Jamie

said. 'Years ago, surgeons used to operate to correct talipes, but it wasn't that effective and it led to problems when the babies grew up. Nowadays we use something called the Ponseti method. What that means is that we'll move and stretch Willow's feet until they're in a better position, then put her feet in plaster casts—that gives her muscles and ligaments a chance to relax and it means the bones grow into the right position. We'll see her every week to soak the casts off in a bath, move her feet again, and redo the casts. It usually takes about six changes of cast until her feet will be in the right position, and then we'll do the operation to release her Achilles tendons. It's really minor—we'll do it under a local anaesthetic so she'll be awake and you won't have to worry quite so much. Then we'll put the last casts on, and three weeks later we'll take them off.'

'Casts.' Kirsty looked anxious. 'She's a week old today.'

'And she's beautiful,' Jamie said. 'I know it's daunting, but this is the best way to help her.'

'You need to keep the casts dry,' Anna said, 'so you'll need to top-and-tail her rather than bath her while the casts are on. But other than that, the casts won't affect Willow's development in any way. You can do everything else that people normally do with babies.'

'Once we've taken off the final casts,' Jamie said, 'we'll give her special boots to wear. They're joined together with a bar, and she'll need to wear them all the time for the next three months, except when she's in the bath, to make sure her feet stay in the right position.'

'And she won't have to wear them any more after that?' Kirsty asked.

'Not all day,' Anna explained, 'but she will need to wear them at night until she's four.'

'Until she's *four*?' Kirsty looked horrified.

'It'll be normal for her, because she won't remember anything else,' Jamie reassured her. 'But it's really effective and it means her feet will develop completely normally—she won't need an operation.'

'I never even had a broken arm as a kid,' Kirsty said. 'To be honest, this whole thing...' She grimaced. 'I wish I'd asked my mum to come with me.'

'The first time's all going to be new for you,' Anna said, 'and the unknown is always

scary. Next time, you'll know what to expect
from the appointment, so it won't be so bad.
You can keep cuddling Willow while we do
the casts, and sometimes it helps to feed a
baby while we're doing the manipulation, to
distract them a bit.' She smiled. 'Talk to her,
sing her a song—I'll sing with you, if that
will help.'

Jamie discovered that not only did Anna
sing beautifully, she knew a lot of lullabies.
Clearly she'd practised them on her nieces,
nephews and godchildren. He remembered
then she'd said that she brought her guitar in
to sing Christmas songs on the ward.

Once Willow's casts had been sorted out
and they'd seen their patients on the rest of the
list for the morning's clinic, they popped in to
see Lily Brown before she went home—and
Jamie was as thrilled by her progress as Lily
herself was—and then grabbed sandwiches
in the hospital canteen.

'So how did you get on at the weekend?'
she asked.

'Really well,' Jamie said. 'I'm seeing my
other sister and my parents next weekend. And
it feels good to be properly back in touch with
them—all thanks to you.'

'Hey, I'm not the one who actually *did* something,' she said with a smile. 'That's all you.'

But she'd given him the confidence to make that move.

He took a deep breath. 'You know you asked me to the Christmas concert with your nieces and nephews tomorrow—I was wondering, is the offer still open, or is it too late to change my mind?'

'Absolutely the offer's still open,' she said, looking pleased. 'I can get one of my sisters-in-law to organise a seat.'

'Then thank you, I'd like to take you up on that.'

'Are you sure?' she asked, looking slightly worried.

No, he wasn't. But he wanted to make the effort. 'Sure,' he fibbed. And he'd fake it until he made it, if it meant that she'd smile at him like that.

'We're all going back to my parents' afterwards,' she said, 'so I hope you'll come with us. Mum will have jacket potatoes baking in the oven, salad prepared in the fridge and chilli in the slow-cooker, and she'll grill chipolatas and vegetarian nuggets for the kids.'

'That sounds lovely,' he said, meaning it. 'Can I bring anything?'

'No, just yourself,' she said. 'We can go straight from work.'

'OK. That's fine.'

Jamie spent Wednesday in Theatre. His final operation of the day was sorting out Michael Jeffries's knee—and thankfully it was Michael's mum who was waiting for him, rather than his dad.

'I'm pleased to say the operation was a success,' he said, when Michael was in the recovery room, 'and he's coming round now.'

'That's great. Thank you so much. What can I do to make things easier for him now he's had the operation?' she asked.

'Keep him topped up with pain medication and get him to be sensible about physio—enough to get him mobile, but not so much that he sets himself back,' Jamie said.

She nodded. 'Football's his life. Sometimes I think it's because my ex—' She paused. 'Sorry. You don't need to know about that.'

'It's fine,' Jamie said. 'Relationships can be tricky. We did wonder if Michael was pushing himself because he loves football or for another reason.'

'He loves football, but mainly because he thinks it'll make his father love him. Whereas my ex just likes to be in control and he changes the goalposts all the time.' She sighed. 'He insisted on taking Michael to that appointment—I was called into work on an emergency and I was hoping Michael's gran would go with him, but unfortunately his father chose to go. I'm sorry if he wasn't very nice to your colleague.'

'Michael told you?'

She shook her head. 'My ex made a few comments about uppity women when he dropped Michael home.'

'Anna's very professional,' Jamie said with a smile, 'but outside the hospital I really wouldn't fancy his chances in a battle of wits against her.'

Michael's mum grimaced. 'Please apologise to her for me.'

'No apology needed,' Jamie said. 'I'm going to be completely unprofessional now. She'll be very glad to learn that Michael's with you and that you put his needs first.'

'I get what you're not saying,' Michael's

mum said. 'And you're right. Thank God Michael lives with me and not his dad.'

'With you on his side,' Jamie said, 'he's going to be just fine. Give it another ten minutes, and you should be able to see him and then we'll settle him onto the ward.'

At the end of his shift, he went in search of Anna. 'I'm ready when you are,' he said.

'Great. How did your ACL repair go?'

'Fine.' He paused. 'Michael's mum is really nice. The first thing she asked me was how she could make things easier for him post-op.'

'Stick gaffer tape over his father's mouth before he says something obnoxious?' Anna suggested.

Jamie laughed. 'And there was me telling her how professional you are.'

She gave him a speaking look. 'I just hope that man doesn't push Michael into undoing all the good work you put into his knee.'

'He won't,' Jamie said. 'Something tells me Michael's mother will be very careful about his visitors.'

'Ah,' Anna said, clearly picking up the subtext.

'She asked me to apologise to you. For Michael's dad.'

'No apology needed. But that's nice of her.' Anna rolled her eyes. 'Right. Let's go and do something really Christmassy.'

'I'm looking forward to it,' Jamie said.

She glanced at him when she'd collected her stuff from the staffroom. 'What's in that bag?'

'That's for me to know, and you to find out later,' he said with a grin.

'Just so you know,' she said on the way to the concert, 'I haven't told my family much about you. Just that you're my colleague and my friend.'

Not a widower they needed to pity and tip-toe round; that was good. But did that mean he wasn't going to get to hold her hand?

Maybe he'd accidentally said it aloud, because she slipped her fingers into his. 'They're all nice, and they won't be nosy,' she said.

'Thank you.'

Her phone pinged on the way there. 'Everyone else is already there and they've saved us two seats,' she said when she checked the message.

'That's kind of them,' he said. 'So how long does the concert last?'

'Maybe an hour. Each class does one piece, and it's just lovely. You always get children singing out of key, forgetting their lines or going off at a tangent, but that's all part of the charm. They all work so hard. What I like is going back year after year and seeing them grow up and change. I've been to all of the school Christmas concerts since Will was in the Reception year and was an angel in the nativity—and his halo fell off.' She grinned. 'We've all learned a lot more about tinsel and sticky tape since then.'

When they walked into the school hall, Anna scanned the rows. 'There they are. Second row on the left. We're right at the end.'

She quickly introduced him to everyone: her parents Tony and Alison; her brothers Mark, Luke and Philip and their wives Susan, Barb and Gemma; her sister Jojo and her wife Becky; and the children who weren't performing that evening, eight-year-old Will, two-year-old Noah, and six-month-old Ivy.

'Nice to meet you all,' he said politely.

'And you, Jamie.' Alison passed him a folded A4 sheet. 'This is the running order,' she said.

'Thank you,' he said.

'Aria's up first,' Anna said, glancing over the sheet with him.

The headmistress began by welcoming them all to the First School's Christmas concert and praising the children for working so hard as a team. 'And now, presenting the Nativity, is our Reception year group,' she said.

'Aria's the third shepherd on the left,' Anna whispered as the children filed onto the stage, slipping her hand into Jamie's.

And it was charming, the story of the nativity told from the donkey's point of view. Jamie couldn't help smiling as the children sang 'Little Donkey' and 'Twinkle, Twinkle, Little Star'; he glanced at Anna and saw she had tears in her eyes. Was she thinking about what might have been, the same way he was?

'OK?' he whispered.

She nodded. 'This is just so lovely. I'm so proud of her.'

Tears of joy rather than tears of pain, then. Reassured, he sat back to enjoy the show.

Two of the Reception children came to the front of the stage while the others filed off.

'I say, I say, I say,' the little girl said. 'What do Santa's helpers learn at school?'

The little boy looked at her. 'I don't know. What do Santa's helpers learn at school?'

'The Elf-a-bet!' she said, and they both giggled.

Jamie couldn't help laughing, too, because their giggles were so infectious.

'And now we have class 1C, singing "The Twelve Days of Christmas",' the headmistress said.

'Megan's class,' Anna whispered. 'She's the partridge.'

Twelve children sat cross-legged on the front of the stage; one little girl stood in the centre of the stage; and the rest stood at the back. The girl in the centre sang the first line about her true love sending her a gift on the first day. Then, as the rest of the children sang what the gift was, Megan lifted a large card showing a hand-drawn partridge in a pear tree.

As the song continued, each child held up their card in turn and lowered it again as the rest of the class sang their way through the gifts, in a kind of Mexican wave. There was a moment of confusion when the geese and swans went up at the same time, but the children recovered themselves quickly and kept singing.

There was another joke during the class changeover—where Jamie learned that lions sang 'Jungle Bells' at Christmas, and then the next class sang 'Jingle Bells', complete with jingling bells; Jamie found his foot tapping along in time. Anna clearly noticed, because she squeezed his hand and grinned at him.

Just as with the previous class, while most of the children filed off the stage two came forward to tell a joke. Jamie stored it away for future reference on the ward: Who says *Oh-oh-oh*? Father Christmas, walking backwards!

'That's so going to be you,' Anna whispered.

Yes. He rather thought it might be heading that way.

The next class sang 'When Santa Got Stuck Up the Chimney,' complete with exaggerated sneezes, and there was another joke before Charlie's class came onto the stage. Most of the class were standing at the back and the sides of the stage, but six of the children were dressed in brown leggings with red tops; they each sported home-made brown cardboard wings, with orange cardboard 'feet' stuck to their plimsolls, and were wearing an orange beak held on with thin elastic.

'Charlie's the one on the far right,' Anna whispered.

While most of the class sang the song about robins, the six 'robins' did a dance in the centre of the stage.

Disaster struck halfway through, when the elastic on the beak of the robin next to Charlie snapped and the beak fell to the floor. The little girl burst into tears, but Charlie was quick to take his beak off and put it on her, then held his hand up to his face to make it look like a beak and improvised.

The little girl stopped crying, everyone cheered, and the dance and song continued.

And that was when Jamie could see exactly where Anna fitted into her family: they were clearly all the same, people who cared about others and helped and made the world of everyone around them a better place.

'Your nephew is amazing,' he whispered.

'I know,' she whispered back.

And Charlie's parents looked so proud of him; Jamie, who didn't even know him, felt proud of him, too.

Jamie learned that Frosty the Snowman

went to school on an icicle. And he didn't even need to look at the programme to guess what the next performance was: a rendition of 'Frosty the Snowman'.

The last performance from the Year Two classes was 'The Little Drummer Boy'; the first class from Year Three recited a number of poems about snow, with some of them using triangles and jingle bells as sound effects.

Hestia, Jamie thought, would probably have suggested some snowflakes dancing on the stage, and given up her free time to coach them.

'That's my new favourite joke,' he whispered to Anna after the next one. 'Why is it so cold at Christmas? Because it's in Decem-*brrr*!' He grinned. 'That's genius.'

The second Year Three class sang 'In the Bleak Midwinter', and followed it up with a joke: 'What do reindeers hang on their tree? Horn-aments!'

'I'm so telling that one in the staffroom tomorrow,' Anna whispered. 'Don't you dare steal the punch line.'

The final class in Year Three sang 'Rudolph the Red-Nosed Reindeer', and Jamie was surprised and impressed to see that the class used sign language as they sang.

The headmistress brought the evening to a close and the whole school sang 'Away in a Manger'; when he glanced round, Jamie could see that most of the parents were close to tears. He had a lump in his throat, too.

Would Giselle's first Christmas concert have been like this?

He could imagine how proud Hestia would have been, how his parents and hers would both have had tears in their eyes for that final carol. And, even though it hadn't turned out that way for him, he was glad he'd shared tonight with Anna and her family. This was something special.

Anna was special, too.

Though he didn't quite know how to tell her.

Once the children had all joined their parents and they'd worked out who was going in whose car, Anna pointed out that there wasn't actually enough room for her and Jamie to squeeze in. 'We'll walk,' she said. 'And, with all this traffic, I bet we beat you home.' She smiled at Jamie. 'It's not raining, so it's actually quite a nice walk from here.'

'Fine by me,' he said, and let her lead him away from the school.

'So what did you think of the concert?' she asked.

'It was lovely,' he said. 'And your nephew— what an amazingly big-hearted boy he is.'

'Yeah. Charlie's pretty special,' she said. 'But I guarantee you all of them would've done the same in his shoes.'

'Because that's who your family is,' he said softly. 'You're all fixers. Which is just lovely.'

'I did tell you that my family's nice.'

He noticed she'd gone pink with pleasure, and he couldn't resist stealing a kiss.

'It was lovely how inclusive the concert was, too,' he said. 'I was amazed by them using sign language for that last song.'

'One of the girls in that class is deaf,' she said. 'Her sister is in Megan's class. And it's really nice because all the others look out for her and they make sure she hasn't missed anything.' She smiled. 'The school's got a really positive attitude when it comes to inclusion and diversity. Although all the children have the option not to take part in something that isn't to do with their particular religion, everyone ends up doing everything because they all want to share. Everyone's included. So as well as the Christmas concert, they learn about Hanukkah, Eid, Diwali and the Chinese New Year, and there are all kinds of activities everyone can take part in.'

'Tolerance, kindness and understanding are all good things. They stop fear and hatred building,' he said.

'Agreed,' she said fervently.

They reached Anna's parents' house almost at the same time as her brother's car pulled outside and her dad hopped out to open the front door.

'Told you it'd be as quick to walk home,' Anna teased.

'Indeed, Anna-Banana.' Her father gave her a hug.

What seemed like only seconds later, the house was full of people chattering and children laughing, and Jamie was swept right into the middle of it.

'For us?' Alison said when he handed her the large bag he'd been carrying.

'My contribution to tonight,' Jamie said.

She opened it, drew out the enormous tub of chocolates and gave him a hug. 'Thank you, sweetheart. These will go down really well later.'

And, just like that, he realised that they'd accepted him as Anna's friend and he was more than welcome to be part of them. He felt another crack open in the mortar of the wall he'd spent years building around him; and he was shocked to realise that, rather than making him want to build that wall higher, it made him want to start dismantling it.

Just as Anna had told him, there was an assortment of jacket potatoes, chilli, chipolatas, vegetarian nuggets and salad for dinner, followed by fruit, trifle, mince pies and chocolate cake for pudding.

And then the children annexed him. 'We need to teach you the robin dance,' Charlie said, and Jamie found himself hopping about like a robin, flapping his wings and dancing with them all as they sang the song.

After that, the games began in earnest.

'Can we play Simon Says next?' Megan asked.

'Except at this time of year we call it Santa Says,' Will added. 'Will you be Santa, Jamie? Please?'

'I'll *pretend* to be Santa,' Jamie said, 'because the real Santa's obviously really busy right now, getting everything ready to be loaded onto his sleigh.' He glanced at Anna and saw that her eyes were bright with approval. 'Though Santa always needs helpers,' he added, giving her a pointed look.

'Auntie Anna-Banana!' the children chorused.

'Come and help, Auntie Anna,' Will said. 'Please.'

'All right. Santa's helper, that's me,' she said, and came to stand beside him.

'Santa says,' Jamie announced, 'hop like a robin.'

The children all hopped delightedly, whooping and giggling, while all the adults perched on chairs and sofas, watching them.

Anna coughed. 'Oi, you lot. The only ones who get a free pass on this are Mum and Dad. The rest of you—on your feet, right now,' she demanded.

With much mock-grumbling, Anna's brothers and sisters joined the children, and everything got rowdier and funnier. Anna joined Jamie with suggestions of things that Santa would do: delivering a present, sliding down the chimney, feeding a carrot to the reindeer, eating a mince pie. The adults were caught out, one by one; in the end, Megan won the game, and Anna presented her with a sparkly reindeer headband.

'Where did you magic that from?' Jamie whispered.

'Christmas fair,' she whispered back.

Alison brought in her whiteboard from the kitchen, Becky drew a very impressive reindeer in about ten seconds flat, and someone else produced a scarf to be tied round the contestant's eyes in a game of Put the nose—a round red magnet—on Rudolph.

This time, Aria won, and was thrilled with her prize of a cuddly snowman.

Anna had felt slightly guilty about not warning Jamie what family evenings turned into at her parents' house; she should've given him the chance to back out of dinner, in case all the games and closeness with the children were too much for him. But he really seemed to be enjoying it, taking part in all the games. In the Who am I? game, where you had a picture of your character stuck on your reindeer antlers and asked questions to help you guess what you were—when the answers could only be 'yes' or 'no'—Jamie cheated horrendously by mouthing questions to Charlie, who won triumphantly. To her surprise, Jamie was the one to suggest boys versus girls for a game where paper cups were stacked in a pyramid and you had to knock them over with a ball made out of socks, where Will won and everyone commented on how many times Anna could miss the entire stack and speculated on whether she'd be able to hit the enormous Christmas tree with the ball if she was standing right next to it. And he sat down and cuddled Ivy and Noah, finishing off by reading one of Aria's favourite stories with all the children gathered round him.

'He's a keeper,' Jojo said quietly to her. 'We all think so.'

'We're not dating,' Anna whispered back.

'Liar,' Jojo said. 'But we really like him. So do the kids. And I love the fact that he makes you smile.'

'It's very early days,' Anna warned.

'Even so. Be happy, my lovely big sister,' Jojo said. 'You deserve this.'

When Jamie had finished the story, he closed the book. 'And that's it, I'm afraid. I have to go now because I need an early night.

I'm doing operations at the hospital tomorrow morning.'

'At Auntie Anna-Banana's hospital?' Charlie queried.

'Yes,' Jamie said with a smile. 'We work on the same ward.'

'Will you come back and play with us again?' Aria asked.

'Yes, if you'll have me,' Jamie said.

'Or we could come to your house and play *your* games,' Megan said with a wide, wide smile.

'Meggie, you're supposed to wait to be invited to someone's house,' Will intervened.

'But Jamie's our friend now,' Megan argued, 'and you're allowed to ask to go to a friend's house.'

'We'll sort something out,' Jamie said. 'Soon.'

'Pinkie-swear?' Megan asked.

'Pinkie-swear,' he said.

Oh, how easy it would be to fall in love with Jamie Thurston, Anna thought. And the way he'd been with her family tonight, chatting easily to all of them and not minding the kids taking over...

He caught her eye. 'Shall I walk you home?'

'That'd be good,' she said.

Once they'd said goodbye to her family and had walked a few steps down the street, Jamie took her hand.

'I'm sorry,' she said. 'I should've warned you that the kids can be a bit full on.'

'Let's just say I can see exactly who their aunt is,' he said.

She winced. 'Sorry.'

'Don't apologise. They're nice. And, yes, it was very full on. But it meant I didn't get a chance to… Well, brood, I suppose, and think of what might have been. It was good for me to go with the flow.'

'And how. I can't believe how badly you cheated at Who Am I?—putting questions in Charlie's mouth.'

'Your dad was doing the same with Megan,' he pointed out, 'and Aria had her dad *and* your sister coaching her.'

She laughed. 'Yeah.'

'I enjoyed it,' he said. 'Your family's lovely. I really appreciate the way they just accepted me for who I am, not asking any questions.'

'They liked you,' she admitted.

He met her gaze. 'Good,' he said softly.

He led her down the next road.

'This isn't the way back to my flat,' she said.

'I know. It's the way to mine. Come in for a coffee,' he said.

She really hadn't expected that. He was actually letting her into his inner sanctum. 'Thank you. I'd like that.'

His flat was incredibly tidy—and incredibly impersonal, she thought. Unlike hers, his fridge was unadorned by magnets holding up children's drawings or photographs; the only thing out on the kitchen worktops was a kettle. It was worse than a show home, because it didn't even pretend to be a home: it was simply somewhere to exist.

'You'd put one of those decluttering experts to shame,' she said lightly.

'It's a short-term let.' He shrugged. 'So it makes sense to keep things tidy.'

It was a very clear warning that Jamie was planning to move on in a few weeks. She shouldn't let herself fall for him, no matter how lovely he'd been with her family or how much she liked him. They didn't have a future—and wishing wouldn't make things different.

'Uh-huh,' she said.

Once he'd made them both a mug of coffee, he ushered her through to the living room. There were no pictures, no books, no music, she noticed. The only personal thing in evidence was a silver picture frame on the mantelpiece containing a wedding photograph. Unable to stop herself, she went over for a closer look.

Jamie was wearing a traditional tailcoat and a top hat, and Hestia was wearing a timeless and very elegant white dress; they were standing in front of the doors of an ancient country church. It was the sort of photograph you saw illustrating bridal magazines, she thought. The perfect couple at their perfect wedding.

'Hestia was very beautiful,' Anna said. And her total opposite: slender, petite and blonde.

Both Jamie and Hestia were practically shining with happiness, clearly deeply in love with each other, and she felt a pang for him. For what should have been.

'It's a gorgeous photo,' she said, and replaced it on the mantelpiece. 'Sorry. I shouldn't have been prying.'

He smiled at her. 'Don't apologise. You weren't prying. Given that I don't keep knick-knacks around, I guess it makes the photo a bit of a focal point.' He paused. 'Would you rather I turned it to the wall?'

'No, of course not. Hestia was your wife and you loved her.'

He nodded. 'We were together for ten years.'

'It's a long time to love someone, and whatever happens in your future she'll always be part of your life.'

'I don't have any regrets about our time together. Just for the stuff we didn't get a chance to do,' he said. 'For you, it must be harder.'

'Sometimes, but I try to remember the good times with Johnny,' Anna said. 'Because there were a lot, especially in the early years. It's just a shame that...' She shrugged. 'Well, life isn't perfect. You need to make the best of what you have, whether that means making a big change or finding a compromise. Look for the happiness.'

'Come and sit with me,' he said softly. 'If it doesn't make you feel awkward.'

She appreciated the fact that he was so sensitive. 'No, I don't feel awkward.' She joined him on the sofa. 'You said this was a temporary place.'

'I've rented it for the length of my contract at the hospital,' he said.

So was that what he did? Rented somewhere temporarily while he was a locum, and then moved on?

'Nalini's maternity leave is going to be for longer than three months,' she said. 'Would you consider staying for a bit more of it?'

'Maybe,' he said.

She winced. 'Sorry. I'm being pushy again.'

'Being direct,' he said with a smile. 'Which is good for me. It stops me ducking the issue.'

Though he rather had ducked the issue, she thought. He hadn't actually said he'd consider staying for longer. And he'd mourned Hestia and their daughter for three years now. Would he ever be ready to move on? And, if so, would he choose to move on with her? Or was she hoping for too much?

The one thing that really troubled her was the issue of children. Even if Jamie was ready to move on, would her infertility mean that she wasn't going to be enough for him? Because there were no guarantees that IVF would work. She might not be able to offer him the future he really wanted, if that was a future with children.

So did that mean she'd be a stepping stone for him—just as he could be a stepping stone for her, to help her move on from Johnny's betrayal? Maybe that would work; they could be each other's transitional partner, easing each other from the pain of the past so they were ready for happiness in the future. Except in that case she'd have to keep some emotional distance between them and not let herself fall in love with him, because it was way too much of a risk to let herself fall in love with a man who wouldn't want a future with her. It would be setting herself up for even more heartbreak.

But was a temporary relationship, one with all her barriers up, enough? Would she be able to stop herself falling in love with Jamie? Had she already started to fall in love with him?

She didn't have a clue.

So all she could do was make the most of the moment, and enjoy being curled up on the sofa with him.

CHAPTER NINE

ON FRIDAY MORNING a case came in that made Anna worry and go to Jamie's office.

'Everything all right?' he asked when she knocked on his door.

'I need your input,' she said. 'The Emergency Department's sending up a six-month-old baby with a femoral shaft fracture.'

He went very still. 'Are we looking at a safeguarding issue?'

'Not sure,' she said. 'Before we see Zac and his parents, can we take a quick look at the X-rays?'

'Sure.'

She pulled up the X-rays on his screen and he peered at them.

'It's not the only fracture,' he said. 'There are others that have healed.'

She took a deep breath. 'So is it safeguarding?'

'Possibly not,' Jamie said. 'His bones seem quite short. How much does he weigh?'

'He's right on the fiftieth centile—eight kilos.'

'That's a pity,' he said. 'I was hoping we could send him for a DEXA scan, but he needs to weigh ten kilos before we can do that.'

She looked at him. 'DEXA scan? You're thinking OI? But there isn't a family history. The Emergency Department already asked about that.'

'A quarter of cases of osteogenesis imperfecta are new ones,' Jamie said. 'Do you want me to come with you?'

'Yes, please,' she said.

She introduced them both to Zac's parents, who were both white-faced and looking anxious.

'I can't believe he's got a broken leg,' Zac's mum said. 'He hasn't rolled off anything—I never leave him on the baby-changer unsupervised. How can he have broken his leg?' She bit her lip. 'I thought it might be a tummy thing because he wasn't feeding properly. That's why I took him to see the doctor. He hasn't been crying or anything.'

'And we haven't done anything to him.'

Zac's dad looked panicky. 'We'd never hurt him. And we haven't left him with anyone who'd hurt him. I don't understand.'

'I know they've already asked you downstairs,' Anna said gently. 'We have guidelines and protocols. Our duty is to our patients.'

'We get that,' Zac's mum said. 'But it's not very nice, people thinking we've hurt him.'

'His X-rays show other fractures that have healed,' Jamie said.

'Other fractures?' Zac's dad looked horrified. 'How?'

'Oh, my God. This whole time I thought he was a fussy eater, but he's been in pain and we didn't know. He's not a crier. I…' Zac's mum was close to tears.

'Can we examine Zac?' Jamie asked.

She nodded.

'Hello, little man.' Jamie's voice was calm and soft. 'Let's have a look at you.' He blew a raspberry at the baby, undressed him down to his nappy, and gently moved his arms and legs. There was no sign of bruising, Anna noticed, but his movements were slightly different from those of most of the babies she saw. And the whites of Zac's eyes were bluer than normal. Both symptoms supported

Jamie's suggestion of a diagnosis of osteo-genesis imperfecta.

'Let's get you wrapped up again,' Jamie said gently, 'so your mum and dad can give you a cuddle.'

'You don't think we're hurting our boy?' Zac's dad asked, his voice cracking.

'No. I think,' he said, 'that Zac has a con-dition called osteogenesis imperfecta, or OI for short. You might also have heard it called brittle bone disease.'

'But—nobody on either side of our family has anything like that. They asked us down-stairs,' Zac's mum said. 'And when we told them it couldn't be, they started looking wor-ried and…'

'…and that's why they sent you up to see us,' Jamie said. 'A quarter of people we see with OI don't have a family history. What it means is that the collagen—that's the protein responsible for bone structure—is of lower quality than average, so it can't support the minerals in the bone and that means the bones fracture a lot more easily than usual.'

'So that's what's caused his broken leg? It's nothing we've done wrong?' Zac's mum asked.

'It's nothing you've done wrong,' Jamie confirmed. 'Why I wanted to examine Zac just now was to see how his joints moved. They're very flexible—something we call hypermobility—and I noticed on the X-rays that his bones seem shorter than usual.'

'The whites of his eyes are bluer than average, too, which is another sign of the condition,' Anna said.

'Is it…? Will he…?'

Jamie clearly guessed what Zac's father was struggling to ask. 'It's a serious condition and Zac will need extra support,' he said, 'but it doesn't mean he's going to die young.'

Zac's parents were both pale with relief.

'Can it be treated?' Zac's mum asked.

'Yes. We'll give him some Vitamin D supplements because it helps the body to absorb calcium and make bone. We'll also give him a special drug to help his bone density,' Jamie explained, 'and we'll measure his bone density regularly with something called a DEXA scan. It doesn't hurt, though he'll need to lie still for a minute or so during the scan and it's a good idea not to have metal fastenings on his clothes.'

'We'll remember,' Zac's dad said.

'The main thing is to manage fractures and manage the risk. We'll be able to sort out the fractures with casts, splints and a brace, but we also need to make sure he's still mobile. If he doesn't move enough, it will weaken his bones and muscles and lead to further fractures,' Jamie said. 'When he's older we might put metal rods in his long bones for support. You can get expandable ones that we lengthen with magnets, so he won't need an operation to replace the rods.'

'Swimming and water therapy will be really good exercises for him, as they lower the risk of getting a fracture,' Anna added.

Zac's mum smiled wryly. 'So he's not going to do what his dad hoped and become a prop forward for the Welsh rugby team.'

'He's still going to be able to wave a flag and sing the songs,' Zac's father said. He stroked Zac's cheek. 'But basically anything we do might hurt him. That's absolutely terrifying. We don't want him to get any more broken bones or be in pain. We want to keep him safe.' He bit his lip, shaking his head in obvious anguish. 'How do we manage things so we don't accidentally hurt him?'

'Slow, gentle movements so you don't startle him,' Anna said, 'because if he moves suddenly he could end up with a fracture. But you can rock him, cuddle him, talk to him and sing to him just like you do with any other baby—just be gentle and support him as much as you can.'

'When you lift him, make sure his limbs and his fingers aren't caught in a blanket,' Jamie said. 'Make sure your hands are wide when you lift him: one under his buttocks and lower back, and the other behind his head and neck.'

'You might need to change your nappy-changing technique a little bit, too,' Anna said. 'Don't lift him by his ankles.'

'Is that how we broke his leg?' Zac's mum asked.

'It could've been several things,' Jamie said. 'A baby doesn't always cry when a fracture happens. You might just notice a bit of swelling around a limb—or, as you did when you took him to be checked over, that he's not feeding well. The main thing is to remember that it isn't your fault. No matter how careful you are, a fracture can still happen.'

'So when you change his nappy,' Anna said, 'slide your hand under his buttocks to lift him.

You might find it's useful to put a clean nappy under him first and then remove the dirty one, so you only have to lift him once.'

'Do you feed him by breast or bottle?' Jamie asked.

Zac's mum grimaced. 'Bottle. I know breast is meant to be better, but...'

'It's fine,' Jamie reassured her. 'You might find it helpful to put him on a pillow when you feed him, and make sure you change sides each time you feed him so he gets used to turning his head both sides.'

'What about winding?' Zac's dad asked. 'Oh, my God. My mum pats him on the back. That's going to damage his spine, isn't it?'

'It could cause problems, yes,' Jamie said. 'Colic drops are a better way of managing wind for Zac.'

'And drying him after a bath. Mum says you have to pat a baby dry,' Zac's mum said. 'So we might've broken his leg that way. Oh, my God.'

'Use a support sponge in the bath,' Anna said. 'And you could try drying his creases with a hairdryer on a cool setting rather than by patting him dry.'

'And dressing him. Those sleep suits. You

have to wrangle him into them, sometimes.' Zac's dad looked horrified. 'I might've broken his arm. Or that might be how his leg broke.'

'It's worth looking for clothes that open wide so you can put Zac on the clothes, then fasten the outfit around him,' Anna said.

'Maybe Mum can make him something,' Zac's dad said.

'It's a lot to take in.' Zac's mum bit her lip. 'I'm going to be terrified to touch my boy in case I hurt him. But not being cuddled isn't good either. I just… I don't know how to deal with this.'

'We can put you in touch with a support group,' Jamie said. 'Talking to other parents who've been in your situation will reassure you much more than we can.'

'But we do have leaflets as well,' Anna said. 'The main thing is we have a diagnosis so we can make sure everyone supports you— your health visitor, your family doctor, and information for nursery and school as he gets older.'

'Because of the brittle bones, Zac's more likely to have some hearing loss, so he'll need his hearing tested before he starts school and then every three years,' Jamie said. 'We'll get a cast sorted out for his leg now, and you can get in touch with us at any time if you're worried.'

Once they'd finished treating Zac and his parents had taken him home, Anna turned to Jamie. 'Thank you.'

'Hey, you would've had to call me in for the fracture anyway,' he pointed out.

'But you were so good with the parents.'

'I hope so. It's our job.' He smiled at her. 'Are you free for lunch?'

She wrinkled her nose. 'Sadly, I have a hot date with acres of paperwork and a very big mug of coffee. But if you're free this evening, I have an idea.'

'A Christmassy idea?'

'Wait and see.' She tapped her nose.

It was incredibly Christmassy—a carol service at Temple Church, the round Crusader church in the middle of London.

'This is one of my favourite places in the city,' Anna said. 'I love the Crusader effigies here and the little lions and dragon at their feet, and the grotesques in the nave. It's worth looking at them after the service.'

'I've lived in London for most of my life,

but I've never been here before,' Jamie admitted.

'It's not open at the weekend, so you'd have to take a day off to visit,' she said. 'But with my oldest brother being an architect, I've been taken to all kinds of incredible buildings. This one survived the Great Fire of London but it was really badly damaged in the Second World War. But they've done a fabulous job of the restorations.'

'And how,' Jamie said, looking up at the incredible vaulted ceiling. There was a huge Christmas tree in front of the Norman doorway beneath the rose window, scattered with white lights and huge baubles; enormous pillar candles in wrought-iron and glass lanterns lit the choir stalls. The church was absolutely packed, and there was something both peaceful and moving in the sound of the congregation singing carols along with the choir.

It was fine until they got to 'Silent Night'; it had been Hestia's favourite carol and Jamie's throat closed up to the point where he just couldn't sing the first verse.

He sensed Anna glancing anxiously towards him. He really needed to be fair to her. She'd brought him here because it was something she loved and wanted to share with him. So he needed to see the joy in this—to do what she did. He thought of her words to him on Wednesday night. *'You need to make the best of what you have... Look for the happiness.'*

Look for the happiness and be the man he wanted to be instead of letting himself get mired in regrets. In the third verse, he found his voice again and sang along. The words that stuck in his head were 'love's pure light': that was what he could see right here, right now, in the church.

After the service, Anna showed him her favourite grotesques in the nave; and then they filed out with the rest of the congregation.

'Was it...?' Anna's sea-green eyes were wide with worry.

'It was perfect,' he said softly. 'Thank you. And I'm glad I shared it with you. I can't think of anyone else I would rather be with, right now.'

Her eyes filled with tears, and one spilled over.

He wiped it away with the pad of his thumb. 'Anna. Don't cry. I didn't mean to hurt you.'

'You haven't. Just... You looked a bit upset earlier.'

'"Silent Night". It was Hestia's favourite carol.'

'It's mine, too. She had good taste.'

'Yeah.' He took her hand. 'Shall we walk along the river to London Bridge?'

'I'd like that,' she said.

They wandered hand in hand along the Embankment, and all felt right in Jamie's world: as if something had tilted and everything had slid into place. Right here, right now, with this woman, he realised that he was actually happy. That he could see a future, for the first time in a very long while. It wasn't going to be easy, and they'd have to be painfully honest with each other over the question of having a family, but he really wanted to make this work.

He held Anna's hand all the way to London Bridge, all the way to the station at Bank, all the way on the tube until they were back in Muswell Hill, and all the way back to her front door.

'Come in for hot chocolate?' she asked.

Not ready to leave her yet, he agreed.

Except they didn't actually get to making the hot chocolate. Although she put the milk in the microwave to heat through, Jamie spun her into his arms and kissed her. It was sweet and light and frothy at first, but then he nuzzled her lower lip and her lips parted, inviting him to deepen the kiss.

By the time he broke the kiss, his head was spinning.

'Stay with me tonight?' Anna asked, her cheeks pink and her eyes glittering.

How could he resist? 'Yes.'

This time, she kissed him, and the next thing he knew he'd scooped her up into his arms.

'I'm too heavy,' she protested.

'You're perfect as you are,' he said, meaning it. 'Though I do need directions.'

She smiled. 'Right out of the kitchen, second door on the right.

He carried her through to her bedroom, switched on the light, closed the curtains, and then set her down on her feet. 'Are you sure about this?' he asked quietly.

'Very sure,' she said. 'I know we said we weren't going to rush things, but...'

Her smile was shy, and so cute that it broke down the last of his resistance.

He liked Anna. More than liked her. He

was halfway to being in love with her. And it looked as if she felt the same way about him.

So he kissed her. Undressed her. Let her undress him. Made love with her—sensibly, because she had condoms tucked in the drawer of her bedside cabinet. He'd intended maybe to slide out of bed once she was asleep and leave quietly, but he was warm and comfortable and it felt *right* having her curled in his arms. So he gave in to the yearning to stay, and fell asleep with her head on his shoulder and their arms wrapped around each other.

On Saturday morning, Anna woke first.

Oh, help.

They hadn't planned this.

She had absolutely no idea how he was going to react this morning. Would he back away, horrified at losing control? Would he be shy? Or had they both moved past everything to a new understanding?

Before she could worry herself silly about it, his eyes opened.

'Hey,' he said.

And his smile was sweet and warm and everything she could wish for.

'Hey, yourself,' she said lightly. 'I, um...' Then she stopped. What did she say?

'Yeah. I don't know what to say either,' he admitted. 'But I have no regrets about last night.'

Which made everything feel all right. 'In that case,' she said, 'how about breakfast?'

'Wonderful,' he said. 'And I'll help you make it.'

CHAPTER TEN

ON TUESDAY JAMIE was in Theatre all day. He came out to a message from Anna.

Last Christmassy thing to convince you tonight. Meet you at the hospital entrance at five.

Her eyes were sparkling when he joined her at the hospital entrance, so tonight was clearly something she was looking forward to, he thought. But he had absolutely no idea what she'd planned, and she refused to give him a single clue.

When they got off the Tube at Covent Garden, he assumed that it was to see the Christmas decorations. But when she led him through the streets and he saw the iconic building with its glass front, the fan-shaped window and the columns, he stopped and stared. 'The Opera House.'

'Exactly,' she said, smiling. 'There's nothing more Christmassy than a performance of *The Nutcracker*—well, except maybe for a trip to the panto.'

The Nutcracker. Hestia's favourite ballet. The one he'd seen her dance in so many, many, times, as the beautiful Sugar Plum Fairy.

The last ballet she'd danced professionally.

It felt as if someone had just dropped an enormous weight on his head from a great height.

'My best friend and her husband had tickets for tonight, but he's gone down with the flu and she's feeling rubbish, too. She offered the tickets to me, so, I thought we—' She stopped abruptly. 'Jamie?'

'No. I can't do this,' he said. 'I'm sorry, Anna. I just can't.'

She stared at him. 'I don't understand.'

'Because of Hestia.' He took a deep breath. 'She was a ballet dancer. She taught ballet. This was her favourite. The last time I came here, I saw her dance in *The Nutcracker*. So I—I just can't go into the theatre now and watch it. I'm sorry.'

She looked stricken. 'Jamie, I'm so—'

'I need to be on my own,' he cut in. 'It's me,

not you.' The fault was so very much his. 'I'm sorry. I just can't do this. Stay and enjoy the show. The ballet's wonderful. Just… I *can't*.' And then he turned and walked away, before he howled his pain and frustration to the sky.

Anna stared at Jamie's retreating back.

She'd had absolutely no idea that Hestia had been a ballet dancer, or she would never have brought Jamie here.

What she'd planned as a treat, as a lovely surprise that he'd enjoy as much as she would, had turned into an utter nightmare.

She'd never meant to hurt him. She'd thought they'd grown closer since Friday night, when she'd fallen asleep in his arms; they'd spent most of the weekend together, except when she'd had a shift on Sunday and he'd visited his family, and he'd stayed over at her flat again last night. She'd started to think that maybe they had a future.

How very wrong she'd been.

She'd rushed him into this. Too much, too soon.

And she wasn't sure if what they'd had could be repaired. Part of her wanted to go after him, to apologise properly and try to make things right; but he'd been very clear that he wanted to be alone. Going after him and trying to get him to talk might make things even worse. He clearly needed to process things on his own.

She just had to hope that he'd talk to her later, when he'd had a chance to come to terms with his feelings. That they could find some sort of compromise.

What now?

She could just go home.

Jamie had told her to stay and enjoy the show. How could she enjoy it, knowing that she'd hurt him so badly?

Or maybe the music and the show she loved would help her move on from this. Take her away from this misery enough to give her some perspective.

Jamie had also said she was the sort of person who made lemonade when life gave her lemons. She rather thought it would be more like bitter lemon tonight. It was way too late to call anyone else to join her; the show started in fifteen minutes.

So she walked into the foyer, took one of the tickets from her bag, showed it to the usher and found her seat.

The auditorium filled up, and Anna was painfully aware of the empty seat beside her.

Why, why, why hadn't she realised that petite, graceful Hestia would have been some kind of dancer? Why hadn't she guessed that Hestia might've been a ballerina? Why hadn't she asked Jamie to talk more about his late wife?

She felt the sting of tears welling up in her eyes and tried to blink them away. No. She was going to take a step back, enjoy the show for what it was, let the music and the choreography and the costumes take her away from this.

Except it didn't work.

All the way through the performance, she was thinking of Jamie and how she'd virtually scrubbed the top of his scars off with wire wool tonight.

Why hadn't she asked him to go to the ballet with her first? It would still have hurt him, but not as much as this, when he was just faced with it. Why had she stupidly thought that a surprise was a good idea?

And as the sound of the celesta echoed through the auditorium to introduce the Sugar Plum Fairy, the tears slid down her face.

Hestia had been the love of Jamie's life, so it was no wonder that he couldn't recover from the pain of losing her and their baby. How stupid Anna had been to think that they could move on from their pasts together.

And how much Jamie's rejection hurt. She'd kept apart from relationships ever since her marriage to Johnny had imploded; and now, the first time she'd let herself be vulnerable, the first time she'd taken that leap of faith, it had all gone wrong. Right at that moment, she felt as if she'd fallen over the edge of a cliff and her heart had broken into tiny shards all over again.

Stupid, stupid, stupid.

They'd only known each other for a few weeks. So why did this hurt even more than the end of a five-year marriage? Why did it feel as if all the stars had gone out?

She should never have let her barriers down. Never have tried to reach Jamie. Never have let herself believe that she might actually be enough for someone—because she quite clearly *wasn't* enough. All that closeness at the children's Christmas concert, the way Jamie had felt as if he fitted right into her family and her world—it had all been an illusion. An illusion that had shattered along with her heart.

Jamie walked away from the Royal Opera House, thinking of Hestia dancing across the stage as the Sugar Plum Fairy. He was almost oblivious to his surroundings as he headed down the Strand, just putting one foot in front of the other and concentrating on moving away from Covent Garden. Eventually he found himself at Trafalgar Square, with the massive pine Christmas tree covered in white lights, almost guarded by the Landseer Lions and the fountains.

Hestia had loved the National Gallery, too. Van Gogh's *Sunflowers* had been her favourite painting. She'd said it filled her with sunlight.

Swallowing hard, he cut down through Charing Cross to the river. Across the other side of the Thames, the London Eye was lit up, and the Christmas lights shimmered on the South Bank. He walked along the Embankment, past Cleopatra's Needle, and down to Waterloo Bridge. He could hear the Christmassy music from Somerset House; it reminded him of the night that Anna had taken him to the skating rink. The night he'd kissed her accidentally for the first time. When they'd backed off from each other and agreed to be friends.

Except he hadn't been able to resist her warmth and her sweetness.

They'd walked together along the river after the carol concert, hand in hand. He'd been full of peace and joy. The night they'd made love together for the first time.

Right now, everything felt in pieces. The loss and loneliness of losing his wife and his baby, the years of the whole world feeling empty, came back sharply.

Yet Anna had broken through his barriers. She'd filled his world with sunshine just as surely as Van Gogh had filled Hestia with sunshine. She'd taken the sting out of Christmas for him, taught him to find the joy in the lights and the love and the laughter. She'd been so careful to check with him that he was OK with each step, so sensitive and kind—until tonight, when she'd surprised him, though he'd never mentioned Hestia's dancing to her so how was she to have known?

But it wasn't just that she'd taken the sting out of Christmas for him. Being with Anna made the world feel a better place.

He liked her family, and he knew that his family would adore her. Yet here he was, on the verge of throwing it all away and going back to be mired in the misery of his past, focusing on what he'd lost and mourning what might have been.

He could see Anna's face, stricken, when he'd told her that he couldn't go to the ballet with her. She'd been so upset to think that she'd hurt him. It hadn't been her fault. There wasn't a mean or spiteful cell in her body. And he'd hurt her. He'd stamped on the joy she clearly found in *The Nutcracker*—not the same as Hestia's, because Anna enjoyed the ballet as part of the audience rather than performing it. But he'd ignored everything; he'd simply walked away and shut her out.

As he leaned on the railings of the bridge, looking out over the Thames, it started to snow. Tiny flakes, not settling, but still snowing.

Snowflakes.

The Sugar Plum Fairy.

The music he knew so well echoed in his head.

'Hestia,' he whispered. 'Right now I'm lost. I'm lonely. I miss you. I've found someone I can be happy with, and I know you'd be furious with me for being such an idiot right now and letting all that slip through my fingers.'

She didn't answer. Of course not. She couldn't. He knew that. But the music still echoed in his head, as if Hestia was pirouetting through his memories. Meeting her. Falling in love with her. Going to watch her on stage, being spellbound by her grace and the way she could bring a story to life through movement alone. Their wedding day. Learning that they were expecting Giselle. Discovering their baby was a girl. Feeling her kick inside Hestia's stomach, watching his wife bloom with their much-wanted baby.

And then the blackness. The loneliness. The way the world just didn't feel right, whatever he did. The walls climbing higher and higher around him.

And then a tall, smiling woman with sea-green eyes chipping away at the mortar and letting the light through the cracks. Tiny ones at first, growing bigger and bigger. Showing him the joy.

All he had to do was reach out for it. Say yes.

And then he heard it.

The song he always tried so hard to avoid at this time of year.

Before he realised what he was doing, he found himself walking into the square at Somerset House, watching the skaters on the rink. Holding hands, some of them nervously keeping to the edge and some of them showing off more fancy moves.

All he wanted for Christmas…

…was Anna.

The song felt as if Hestia was giving him a hard shove and telling him to move on. To listen to the music. To think about what he really wanted.

'I'll always love you, Hes,' he whispered. And hadn't Anna herself said that he'd always have room in his heart for Hestia because he'd loved her and she was part of him? Warm, generous, lovely Anna—who really didn't deserve to be treated the way he'd treated her. He'd been as selfish as her ex.

'But it's time for me to move on, Hes. You're right. I can't spend the rest of my life in limbo. I want to move on with Anna. I think we could be happy together.' If it wasn't too late. 'You'd like her, Hes. A lot. She's got the same warmth and sweetness that you had, except she isn't you and I don't expect her to be.' He took a deep breath. 'And I've really messed this up. I don't know how to even begin fixing this. I've hurt her and it wasn't fair of me to walk away without explaining.'

The song's words flitted into his head, talking about wishes coming true.

He knew what he wished. That he could move on with Anna. Be with her for Christmas and for always.

Would she let him explain? Would she give him a second chance, even though he'd been so unfair to her?

He glanced at his watch.

Would Anna have stayed to watch the show without him, or would she have gone home?

If he called her, either it would either go to voicemail—telling him that she was still at the Opera House and he had enough time to get back to Covent Garden before the show ended—or she'd be at home and answer.

He hoped.

He grabbed his phone and pressed her number. For a moment, he thought it wasn't going to connect, and then his call went to voicemail.

Please let that mean she was still in the centre of London with her phone switched off, rather than that she was at home and was ignoring his call.

But it would be very easy to miss someone coming out of the Royal Opera House in a crowd. He typed quickly.

I'm sorry. We need to talk. Please will you wait for me by the mistletoe chandelier in the middle of Covent Garden Market?

Please let him not have messed this up too much. Please let her give him a chance.

Crossing his fingers mentally, he sent the text and hurried back to Covent Garden, where he waited by the enormous mistletoe chandelier.

It would serve him right if she left him to wait there. Because he really, really hadn't been fair to Anna. He'd let his past get in the way. It was time to move on, and he wanted to move on now—with her.

He sat on the bench and waited.

And waited.

And waited, while the snow drifted down and started to settle.

Eventually people started to stream past,

some clutching programmes and chattering, telling him that the ballet must have ended.

Would Anna come to meet him? Would she let him apologise and explain? Or had he pushed her away for good?

He waited.

The crowds thinned.

He waited.

There was no sign of Anna.

He glanced at his watch. Maybe she was one of the last out; maybe she'd only just switched on her phone and seen his message; or maybe she wasn't coming.

He'd give her another ten minutes.

Time seemed to have changed its speed; five seconds felt more like a minute.

Nine minutes later, he was starting to think that, yes, he was too late, so he should just give up and go home. Not that his flat was a real home; it was just somewhere to sleep and store his things.

And then Anna came and sat on the bench next to him. 'Hi.'

His heart skipped a beat. She'd come to meet him. 'Anna. I'm sorry. Thank you for coming here.'

'I nearly didn't,' she admitted.

Because she had doubts about him?

As if he'd spoken the question aloud, she said, 'I forgot to turn my phone on again after the show. But I was late out and ended up at the back of the queue for the lift in the Tube station, so I checked my phone while I was waiting. Your message came through just as I was about to walk into the lift.'

'I'm really glad you came.' He took a deep breath. 'I'm sorry. I've been so unfair to you tonight. I've let my past get in the way.'

'Uh-huh.' Her voice was neutral and her face was expressionless.

All he could do was open his heart and tell her how he felt. And hope that it would be enough to make her give him a second chance.

'I walked down by the river when I left you,' he said. 'And I was thinking about Hestia, and about you. You've made my world a different place, Anna. You've given me back something I thought I'd never have again.' He took a deep breath. 'And I won't blame you if you don't want anything to do with me now.

'I should have told you about Hestia being a ballet teacher and dancing in *The Nutcracker*, and I should've thanked you for the opportunity to see the show and gone with you instead of throwing it back in your face and storming off. I've been an idiot. But I've had time to think about it and get my head around things, and I'm so sorry I hurt you.' He took both her hands in his.

'I know we haven't known each other that long, but you make my world feel like a much better place. With you, I see the sunlight. You've taught me to move on—and I want to move on, I really do. More specifically, I want to move on with you.' He looked at her. 'I could hear the music from the ice rink. They played the song I find really difficult, and it made me think about what I wanted. For Christmas and for always. I want *you*, Anna. I love you. Will you marry me?'

Marry him?

Anna stared at Jamie, unable to process this. She thought she'd pushed him away—that he still wasn't ready to move on and she'd hurt him by pushing him too far, too fast. He'd reacted by walking out on her. Would he do that again? Because she didn't want to be in a relationship where she had to second-guess her partner's feelings all the time, be careful what she did and said and tiptoe around certain subjects instead of being completely honest and open.

This wasn't going to be an easy conversation, but she needed to know.

'How do I know,' she said, 'that you won't walk away from me the next time something reminds you of Hestia, of what you lost?'

'You don't,' he said. 'It'll be a risk. But I'm asking you to trust me that I won't make that mistake again. That instead of stomping off I'll talk to you and we'll get past whatever the problem is together.'

That was what she wanted, too: but she still wasn't sure. 'You lost your wife and your baby—and I can't give you a baby. Not without complications, and there are no guarantees that IVF will work. How do I know that I'm enough for you as I am?'

'You're enough for me as you are,' he said.

'Maybe for now,' she said, 'but what about the future? What if you change your mind and decide that you want children?'

'Honestly?' He grimaced. 'I'll warn you in advance, this is going to sound terrible and I don't mean it to be that way.'

'Honesty,' she said, 'is the best thing right now. I need to know what's going on in your head and you need to know what's going on in mine. Pussyfooting around the subject isn't going to work for either of us.'

'OK.' He took a deep breath. 'I was looking forward to being a dad—but losing Hestia and Giselle has left me terrified at the idea of taking that risk again. And, yes, I know the statistics. But there's still a chance it could happen again.'

'So you don't want children.' And then the really nasty thought hit her. 'I can't have children, so that makes me a safe option.'

'That did occur to me at one point,' Jamie admitted, 'and I know how selfish that is. But that's only part of it. I love you, Anna Maskell, for who you are, and it's got absolutely nothing to do with your fertility. And I know you said you've come to terms with not having children, but I've seen the way you are with the kids in your family. I know how family-orientated you are. I think you'd be an amazing mum—so if you want children, then I'll do my utmost to damp down my fears and I'll do whatever it takes to make our family happen. I guess what I'm trying to say is that I love you enough to take a risk that scares me spitless.'

'IVF is a high-risk option,' she reminded him. 'And it might not even work.'

He nodded. 'But if that's what you want, we'll try.' He gave her a wry smile. 'Though if we do try that option and we're lucky enough for it to work, I'll warn you now that you're probably going to have to yell at me for wrapping you up in cotton wool throughout your entire pregnancy.'

'And if the IVF doesn't work?' Would he walk away from her, the way Johnny had?

'If it doesn't work, I'll stay right by your side, and we'll get through the sadness together,' he said. 'IVF isn't the only option. You mentioned that Jenna was a surrogate mum for her sister. We could maybe find a surrogate. Or adopt. Or foster. Or we can just enjoy being an uncle and aunt, and day to day it'll be just the two of us. We have options, Anna.'

'Can it really be that easy?' she asked.

'Yes, it can really be that easy,' he said softly. 'You told me you weren't going to let your infertility define you. It's not going to define us, either. Whether we have children or not, we can still make a family together. You and me. And George the gorgeous goldfish,' he added with a smile.

'How do you know I'm going to be enough for you?' She hadn't been enough for Johnny and, although she'd managed to put the pieces back together, she didn't think she could do that a second time if Jamie walked away from her.

'I know you're going to be enough,' he said, 'because you've brought my world back into colour. You've chipped away at the walls around me and let the light come in. You've shown me that Christmas isn't all about loss— it's about celebrating what you have. Finding the happiness. Finding the joy.'

'I dated Johnny for a year before we got married,' she said. 'I thought he was the one. We were married for five years. And it all went wrong. He walked away from me.' She shook her head. 'I've known you for just over a month, and you walked away from me to-night. How do I know this won't go wrong in the future?'

'You don't,' he said.

She flinched.

'So it means taking a risk. All I can tell you is that you make me feel different. And

I hope I can do that for you—teach you that not all men see the world the same way that Johnny did.'

'We've only known each other for a few weeks,' she said again.

'It's been long enough for me to know,' he said. 'But if you need more time, I'll wait until you're ready. Because you're worth the wait. I love you, Anna. I want you to be happy. I want you to have everything you want in your life—and I hope that starts with me.'

He'd give her the time she needed. Be patient with her.

And she could see in his eyes that he meant it.

He loved her.

He wanted to be with her. He wanted her to want him.

They'd both been through dark times in the past. She'd lost most of her choices over having children and come out the other side of a fractured marriage, having to start her life all over again; and Jamie had buried his wife and baby.

This was their second chance at happiness. Together.

She could walk away from him now, just

as he'd walked away from her earlier this evening.

Or she could see past the hurt, understand why he'd had a wobble, take his hand and step forward to their future.

OK, they hadn't known each other for very long. But they'd worked together, and she liked the way he treated his patients, their parents and his colleagues. They'd spent as much time together as if they'd been dating for several months. And in that short time he'd taught her that she was worth so much more than Johnny had thought. He'd given her her confidence back. They were compatible inside work and outside it, too.

The future wasn't necessarily going to be smooth. But they could support each other through the wobbles, talk things over when they hit a sticky patch. Be honest with each other.

So did she take the risk of telling him how she felt about him and agree to marry him, or should she stay on her own, the way she'd planned?

She looked at him, and the love in his eyes decided her.

'I love you, too,' she said. 'It scares me, because I'd been so determined not to take a risk on anyone ever again. But you've had a tough time, too. And if you're brave enough to take the risk with me, then I'll be brave enough to take the risk with you. So, yes, Jamie, I'll marry you.'

'Good.' He kissed her under the mistletoe. 'And we'll seal another deal, too. You've shown me the joy of Christmas. So I'll gladly wear Santa's red suit on Christmas Day and walk through the ward with a sack of presents, saying, "Ho-ho-ho."' He grinned. 'Or I could walk backwards, saying, "Oh-oh-oh…"'

She laughed, and kissed him back. 'That's a deal.'

CHAPTER ELEVEN

On Christmas Day Anna drew the blinds in Jamie's office and locked the door, then helped him get into the red suit and beard that Robert had left for them.

'You're sure I look the part?' he asked.

'You need a touch more padding, I think,' Anna said. She added another pillow underneath his top, then stood back and eyed him critically. 'Yup, that's it. Perfect.'

'If you'd told me a month ago that I'd be doing this, I would never have believed you,' he said.

'I asked you to do it six weeks ago, and you said no,' she reminded him. 'I'm glad you changed your mind.'

'I see things very differently now,' he said quietly. 'I have you to thank for putting the sunshine back in my life. And now we're going to put a little bit of sunshine into the children's lives. I still think you should've dressed up as an elf.'

'No, because there are children in the ward who would recognise me. And it makes sense to them that Dr Anna will have a special guest on her ward round.'

'Let's do it,' he said, lifting up the sack marked 'Presents'. 'So each bay has its own bag?'

'And every present is named. We've taken turns sorting it over the last week,' she said. 'Teddies for the babies, art stuff for the under-sevens, and age-appropriate books for the over-sevens. A big high-five to the Friends of Muswell Hill Memorial Hospital for raising the funds and buying the presents.'

'Definitely.'

She unlocked the door and led him out.

'Good morning, everyone,' she said to the children in her first bay. 'I have a special visitor to the ward today.'

'Ho-ho-ho. Merry Christmas, everyone,' Jamie said, waving from the doorway. 'Dr Anna, Nurse Sajana and Nurse Keely have agreed to help me give everyone a present.'

'Merry Christmas, Santa!' a little girl called from the corner.

'Merry Christmas!' Jamie called back.

Between them, Anna, Sajana and Keely made sure the right presents went to the right children. Jamie blew everyone kisses, then moved on to the next bay, until every child had a present from Father Christmas.

There were gluten-free mince pies, a big tub of chocolates, mini festive cupcakes, a big tray of cheese straws and a dish of tortilla chips with salsa on the nurses' station in the centre of the department, and as they went through the bays Anna encouraged all the visitors to help themselves.

Anna had brought in her acoustic guitar, and between them she, Keely and Sajana got all the children to join in singing 'Rudolph the Red Nosed Reindeer' and 'Frosty the Snowman', as well as teaching them all the song about robins that Jamie recognised from the school concert she'd taken him to.

Keely's voice was amazing, and Jamie remembered Anna telling him that Keely sang in the hospital's house band, Maybe Baby; she was easily good enough to be professional. Maybe, he thought, the band might sing at his and Anna's wedding next year.

The spirit of Christmas was well and truly alive in Anna Maskell. Peace and love and kindness. She was making a difference to their patients and their families, and she'd made a huge difference to his life.

Quietly, he slipped back to his office and removed the beard and red suit, then came back in his usual clothes to join in with the singing. Even the parents who'd initially looked utterly stressed at having their child so sick that they had to be away from home at Christmas seemed to have relaxed a bit, thanks to Anna.

Finally, at the end of her shift, she came into his office and took his hand. 'Thank you for being so brilliant today.'

'Given how opposed I was to the idea in the first place, I'm blown away by how much I enjoyed it,' he said. 'Seeing them smile and look a bit hopeful, and forgetting how ill they were feeling—just for a little while. If I'm here next year, and Robert wants a break, put me down for being Santa on the ward.'

'Really?'

'Really. I've agreed to cover the rest of Nalini's maternity leave, and after that if she wants to come back part time then we might be able to work out some kind of job-share.'

'That,' she said, 'is the best Christmas present of all.'

He smiled and kissed her. 'No promises. We'll see how it goes. But, even if we don't end up working together when Nalini comes back, we can still try to co-ordinate our shifts in different hospitals.'

'Absolutely,' she agreed. 'Are you sure you're ready for a Maskell family Christmas?'

'I am,' he said. 'And it was amazing of your parents to ask my parents and my sisters to come for Christmas dinner, too.'

She grinned. 'The more the merrier. And everyone's chipping in with desserts and trimmings, so all Mum really has to do is cook the turkey. There's enough room for all the children to run around together and play.' Her grin broadened. 'Dinner and games. It doesn't get more perfect than that.'

'Indeed.' Though Anna didn't know quite *everything,* he thought. As far as she was concerned, the jeweller was still making the pretty engagement ring they'd chosen together, based on a Celtic knot and with a single tanzanite in the centre. He'd had it delivered to her parents the previous day, along with half a dozen bottles of champagne, in strictest secrecy. Because today wasn't just Christmas Day. He'd been exchanging texts with Anna's sister, too, over the last week, and between them they'd come up with the perfect song to go with the delivery of the ring. Jojo had reassured him that it was on her phone, it was on Becky's phone too as a back-up, and she'd play it as soon as he gave her the nod.

He really hoped he'd pitched this right.

When they reached her parents' house, everyone was already there, the children were playing raucous games, a mix of Christmas songs was playing, and the gorgeous scent of Christmas dinner filled the air.

Alison, Anna's mum, greeted them warmly, and Tony, Anna's dad, shoved a glass of wine into their hands.

'Everyone's in the living room,' Alison said. 'Go and say hello.'

'Do you need a hand in here first?' Jamie asked.

'No, because you've both done a full shift already. Go and have fun.' Alison shooed them out of the kitchen.

Jamie and Anna greeted everyone, and were deep in conversation when Tony called, 'Everyone, dinner is about to be served—time to come and sit at the table!'

This was what it felt like to be a part of a big, noisy family again, Jamie thought. And he absolutely loved it.

Everyone chattered during dinner, wearing the paper hats from their crackers and taking it in turn to make everyone else laugh and groan with the cracker jokes.

Jamie helped to clear the table before coffee, but had already primed Mark, Anna's oldest brother, to make her stay put and talk while he was in the kitchen.

Out of Anna's sight, Alison gave him the box to put in his pocket, and he hugged her. 'Thank you so much for helping me.'

'You make my baby happy,' she said simply, 'and that's what matters to me.'

Jojo came into the kitchen and waved her phone at him. 'Ready?'

'I think so.' Though right then he felt incredibly nervous—as nervous as he did before the trickiest operation, all his exams and his driving test, except all rolled into one.

'Hopefully you've practised it enough to know the words,' Jojo said with a grin. 'But Mum, Becky and I will have your back for the chorus.' She ruffled his hair. 'We should've made you put the T-shirt and white trousers on and do it properly, but Anna-Banana loves you anyway so you can get away with it. But you *do* have to dance. That's not optional.'

'Go get your girl, sweetheart,' Alison said, patting his shoulder.

Together, they walked into the dining room, where everyone was still chattering and laughing. Alison tapped a spoon on a glass, and the room fell silent in expectation.

Jojo hit 'Play' and the beginning of 'Wake Me Up Before You Go-Go' came on.

Jamie sang along and danced, not caring that his voice was slightly flat and he couldn't reach the high note on the chorus, because Jojo, Alison and Becky were singing along with him.

He sang the next verse; then, as he'd arranged with Jojo, she stopped the song and he dropped to one knee.

'You *have* chased my grey skies away,' he said, 'and you make the sun shine for me, Anna Maskell. I love you, and I want to wake up with you every day. Will you marry me?' He whipped the box out of his pocket, opened it and held it out to her.

'I don't believe you just did this—and to George,' she said, crying and laughing at the same time. 'Yes! Yes, I'll marry you.'

Everyone cheered, and between them Anna and Jamie's fathers poured the champagne and their mothers poured sparkling grape juice for the children.

'To Anna and Jamie,' Tony said. 'Every happiness. And happy, happy Christmas.'

'Anna and Jamie. Happy, happy Christmas,' everyone chorused.

* * * * *

If you enjoyed this story, check out these other great reads from Kate Hardy

A Nurse and a Pup to Heal Him
Heart Surgeon, Prince…Husband!
Carrying the Single Dad's Baby
Unlocking the Italian Doc's Heart

All available now!